Randal must choose
the real wizard. . . .

The wizard's workroom glowed with an eerie blue light. The illumination came from two overlapping magic circles, laid out on the workroom floor like a pair of linked rings. In the center of each circle stood a wizard.

"Help me!" called the wizard in the circle to Randal's left—a tall, gray-bearded man in ceremonial robes of black velvet embroidered with magical symbols in gold and silver. "Break the circle, so that I can destroy the demon keeping me captive!"

"No!" shouted the other wizard—also tall, also gray-bearded, clad in an identical robe. "No! Help me! *I* am Master Balpesh—he is the demon!"

Randal looked from one wizard to the other. Each stood imprisoned inside a magic circle, holding the other prisoner. They were locked in a deadly stalemate.

"Hurry!" commanded the wizard on the right.

"Free me!" cried the other.

Randal stepped closer to the circles. All he needed to do was put his hand through one circle or the other, and that circle would break. *I have to choose*, he thought. *But I don't dare choose wrong.*

He paused for a moment, then stretched out his hand. . . .

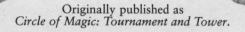

the wizard's apprentice

SECRET OF THE TOWER

Originally published as
Circle of Magic: Tournament and Tower.

Debra Doyle and James D. Macdonald
illustrated by Judith Mitchell

SCHOLASTIC INC.
New York Toronto London Auckland Sydney
Mexico City New Delhi Hong Kong Buenos Aires

*To Mildred Morgan and Larry L. Doyle,
for putting us up—and putting up with us—
when we, like Randal, were on the road*

ISBN 0-439-70363-8

Originally published under the title *Circle of Magic: Tournament and
Tower.* Copyright © 1990 by Scholastic Inc. All rights reserved.
Published by Scholastic Inc. SCHOLASTIC, TROLL, and associated logos
and designs are trademarks and/or registered trademarks of Scholastic Inc.

12 11 10 9 8 7 6 5 4 3 2 1   4 5 6 7 8 9/0

Printed in the U.S.A.   40

First Scholastic printing, October 2004

the wizard's apprentice

SECRET OF THE TOWER

Originally published as
Circle of Magic: Tournament and Tower.

I.

Stableboy

SLAP! RANDAL SWATTED a stinging horsefly that had tried to make a meal from his shoulder.

"One down," he counted aloud. Then he looked at the swarm still hovering in the air around him. "Only about four thousand to go."

The late-afternoon sun beat down on the Basilisk, a small country inn a few days' ride from Tattinham, near the eastern mountains of Brecelande. Inside the stable, the air was thick with the stink of manure and rotting straw, and throbbed with the buzzing of heavy, slow-moving flies. Randal had once been a squire in his uncle's castle of Doun, and most recently had been an apprentice wizard at the Schola Sorceriae, the School of Wizardry, in Tarnsberg on the western sea. Now he heaved another pitchforkload of manure over his shoulder and wondered why he'd ever left home.

Randal was about fifteen, with the height and the sturdy build that come of being well-fed from earliest childhood. At the moment, however, a film of gray dust covered most of his face, and sweat plastered his long, untrimmed brown hair to his head and

1

neck. Soon after a pair of merchants departed, Randal had begun working in the empty stables. The Basilisk's regular hostler—who should have been working with him—had never arrived.

"It's no good," Randal muttered. "I have to rest."

He leaned the pitchfork against the wall of the stable and rubbed his hands down the front of his tunic. His right palm ached, as it did whenever he performed hard physical work these days. He looked down at the hand, at the raised, red scar that stretched across it—low on the side away from his thumb, higher on the other side—so that it actually crossed the first joint of his forefinger.

Randal clenched and unclenched his hand, trying to ease the cramp in the scar-stiffened flesh. If only he hadn't grabbed the sharp-edged blade of Master Laerg's ceremonial sword . . . if only he hadn't used the magical object like a knightly weapon to kill the renegade wizard Laerg before his spells could destroy not only Randal, but the entire School of Wizardry . . . if only . . . but if he hadn't done those things, he would be dead now, and the kingdom of Brecelande would be held fast in Laerg's sorcerous grip.

Even working here for the rest of my life, thought Randal, glancing around the filthy stable, *would be better than that.*

He took up the pitchfork again and returned to mucking out the straw. As he worked, he took some comfort in knowing that tomorrow or the next day should see him on the road again, well away from the Basilisk and its stinking stable, and within reach—at last—of his goal.

Magic.

More than anything else, Randal wanted to be a wizard, a worker in spells and enchantments that could change the texture of reality—or, more practically, make short work of clearing out a filthy stable. He had spent three years at the Schola in Tarnsberg studying the magical arts before he broke the oldest law of wizardry—the one that forbade a wizard to attack or defend with steel.

His action had saved the Schola from destruction, and the Regents—the master wizards who controlled the School of Wizardry—had not been ungrateful. They'd made Randal a journeyman wizard, setting him on the second stage of the long road that led from apprenticeship to mastery. But they'd also done something else.

They'd taken his magic away from him. Until he could get permission from the wizard Balpesh, once a Regent of the Schola and now a hermit living near Tattinham in the eastern mountains, all Randal's skill and training had to remain untouched, no matter how great the need.

Randal slapped at another fly. Back in Tarnsberg, any second-year apprentice could get rid of these flying nuisances with an elementary spell. He could do it himself right now. Nothing prevented him except his own will.

The Regents of the Schola hadn't put him under any kind of enchantment or binding spell when they barred him from the use of magic; they had done something far simpler, and far less kind. They had asked for his sworn word, and he had given it.

A wizard doesn't lie, thought Randal, bending again at his work. *Even if I can't work magic right now, I'm still a wizard. The Regents said so.*

Randal had wanted to be a wizard ever since a master wizard named Madoc the Wayfarer visited Castle Doun. The training that kept Randal true to his promise, however, had begun a long time before. Lord Alyen, who was Randal's uncle and brother of the baron who ruled over Doun, had never spoken an untruth in Randal's hearing—and Sir Palamon, the castle's master-at-arms, who was in charge of turning squires into knights and clumsy peasants into seasoned fighting men, had his own way of dealing with liars and oath breakers.

Sir Palamon, reflected Randal, *had high standards. In everything. If he ever saw this stable, he'd nail the hostler's hide to the wall.*

More than once, on his long journey eastward from Tarnsberg, Randal had caught himself half wishing he had never left the castle and barony of Doun. If he'd stayed, he'd have been almost a knight by now; Sir Palamon himself had said that Randal showed promise.

But no, I had to be smart. Living at ease for the rest of my life wasn't good enough.

Another forkload of manure went over his shoulder.

I wanted to understand the mysteries of the universe.

Randal gulped a breath through his mouth—the air was too nasty to breathe any other way—and

4

dragged the back of his arm across his forehead in a vain attempt to keep the sweat from running into his eyes.

"Mysteries of the universe, hah!" he muttered aloud. "I'm standing knee-deep in the mysteries of the universe right now."

The thought made Randal laugh. In the dusty stable, the laugh turned into a choke, then a coughing fit. He staggered out of the open door into the sweet air and sunlight of the inn yard. He was coughing so hard that he barely heard the ringing of bridles and pounding of hooves as a trio of mounted men swept through the gate and into the yard.

He looked up as the cavalcade blocked the light in front of him. Through watering eyes he got an impression of bright colors and rich patterns. As the coughing fit passed, he heard a voice bellowing in his ear, "Boy! Say, boy! Take care of the horses, I say!"

Randal turned toward the speaker, and saw a young man scarcely a year or two older than himself. The youth wore the belt, spurs, and chain of a knight, and rested one gloved hand on the hilt of a sword.

So this is what they're making knights out of these days, thought Randal. *Sir Palamon was right about chivalry going downhill in a greased handcart.*

The young man wasn't amused by Randal's appraising glance. "Look at me that way again, boy, and I'll slap your eyes out. Now take the horses and be quick about it—their comfort's worth more than your miserable life."

5

Randal looked away. He took the bridles of the horses as they were given to him and kept his thoughts to himself. The Basilisk's regular hostler, the one Randal was supposed to be assisting, came running up to help with the task, all the while bowing to the lordlings and muttering a stream of flattering phrases.

In spite of the hostler's show of eagerness, most of the work still fell to Randal. He walked the horses down, dried them, and curried them. When that task was finished, the hostler had Randal spread new straw and set out hay. By the time the work in the stable was done, the sun had almost set, and Randal had to help close the gates of the inn yard.

With its gates closed and barred, the inn resembled a small fortress more than it did a place where hospitality might be found. Nobody inside the walls complained, however—no honest man went abroad in this country by night. Some folk claimed that in the old days, before the death of the High King, wild beasts were never seen outside of the deepest forests, and a man could walk alone from one side of the realm to the other with a sack of gold tied to his belt, and never fear a thief. But if those days had ever truly existed, they were long gone. When they could, travelers spent the night behind locked doors.

After the gates were shut, Randal went to the kitchen behind the main room of the inn. These days, as he made his way to Tattinham as a traveling laborer, he never got to walk into any place by the front door. In the kitchen, the cook set Randal to

6

scouring out the pots and pans from dinner. Finally, almost two hours later, Randal got his own share of the evening meal: a small portion of burned meat and soggy bread.

He retreated with the food to the chimney corner, where he wolfed down the bread and meat in spite of the taste. As usual, the food vanished long before his hunger was satisfied. He thought wistfully of the meals he'd eaten at the Schola. Like most other apprentices, he had complained about the school's plain and somewhat monotonous fare. But there had always been more than enough to fill even the emptiest stomach.

"If I'd known then what I know now . . ." Randal muttered. The cook shot him a murderous look, and he fell silent again.

After his meal, he made his way across the yard to his sleeping place in the stable. Although the afternoon had been hot, the night breeze blowing through the dark inn yard made Randal shiver. His stomach growled a protest against the scanty meal, but since he couldn't do anything about the emptiness in his midsection, he ignored it.

He couldn't help remembering what Madoc the Wayfarer had said when Randal was still a squire at his uncle's castle, and becoming a wizard had seemed like a bright and wonderful dream: "You'll be hungry more often than fed," the master wizard had told him, "and you'll spend more time in danger on the road than safe under a roof."

Madoc was certainly right about that one, thought Randal. So intent was he on his own thoughts that he didn't watch the path ahead of him. A moment later, he ran straight into a warm, cloth-covered wall.

"Churl!" said a familiar and slightly drunken voice. It was the young knight he'd encountered in the inn yard earlier. "Do you realize you've stepped on the toe of a nobleman?"

Wonderful, Randal thought. *Just the way I wanted to end the day.*

He tried to sidestep the young knight and continue on toward the stable. But the nobleman was not pleased.

"Don't you have a tongue, you insolent oaf? I'll teach you to touch a knight."

"I'm . . . I'm sorry, my lord," Randal mumbled.

"You certainly are," growled the knight. "And you'd be even sorrier if I had the schooling of you."

Randal started to mutter something properly apologetic, but a second voice cut in from behind him and drowned out his words.

"What's all this, then?"

"Not much," said the first knight. "Just a peasant with no manners."

"That so?" said the other. "Turn around, peasant."

Randal felt a hard shove between his shoulder blades. He turned to look at the man who had pushed him. The move turned out to be a serious mistake.

"Boy!" snarled the one who had spoken first. "Do you dare turn your back on a knight?"

Randal felt another hard shove, one that spun him around again in spite of his effort to keep his feet.

8

"No manners at all," said the second man behind him. "He was warned, and here he's turned his back on a knight again. We'll have to teach him." As he spoke, he dealt Randal a slap that made the young wizard's head reel.

Through the buzz in his head, Randal heard a new voice joining in with the others. "What do we have here?"

"A dirty little pig that doesn't know how to act before his betters," said the first knight.

"Time he was taught a lesson, then," said the new voice. Randal felt another blow, harder than the others. This hand wore rings.

Laughter echoed in the night. A foot kicked out and snatched Randal's leg from under him. But Randal knew how to fall, and he rolled quickly back to his feet. He tried to get away and fade into the shadows, but one of his assailants caught him and pushed him into the circle again.

"Don't leave before you're dismissed, boy."

Randal wavered to a stop in front of the knight who had just spoken. His head still spun from the blows he had taken, and he almost lost his balance.

"That's not the way to bow, fool," said the knight.

Randal kept his head down, but his fists at his sides were clenched tight. If only he had his magic back again . . . *It wouldn't even take a lightning bolt, just a flash and a bang and these knights would be running for their lives. But I gave my word.*

A buffet from the clenched fist of his latest tormentor almost knocked Randal off his feet. He clenched his own fists tighter, feeling the pain in his scarred palm and welcoming it as a distraction.

One of the other knights slapped Randal so hard the youth's eyes watered, and his ears rang with the blow.

I could take him, thought Randal through the racket in his head. *I'm not banned from fighting—just from using steel. But if I knock him down, his friends will probably kill me.*

A boot hit Randal in the knee. He collapsed, and this time he stayed on the ground. He rolled into a ball on the packed dirt, hoping to protect himself from serious injury while the group of knights worked off their bad temper.

The next kick did not land. Instead, a deep and somehow familiar voice called out, "Let him go."

I've heard that voice somewhere, thought Randal.

So, it seemed, had the ones who'd been bullying him. He sensed them drawing back away from him, and then heard one of them—the young knight who had started the game—ask in a surly tone, "Who dares command me?"

"Sir Walter of Doun," said the newcomer. "Who asks?"

"Sir Reginald de Haut Desert," said the first knight stiffly, like a dog backing off from its prey when it sees the pack leader coming. "I have heard of you, sir."

And so have I, thought Randal miserably, pressing his head into his knees where he lay in the dust of the inn yard. His cousin Walter was the last person in Brecelande he wanted to see at the moment. Even getting kicked senseless by Reginald and his friends would have been preferable.

"And I have heard of you, sir." Walter's voice was courteous, but unyielding.

There was a pause, and then another voice from the circle around Randal said, "This one isn't worth dirtying my boots on. I'm going back inside."

From the sounds, Randal knew that the others had left with him. Walter spoke again out of the darkness above Randal.

"Here, now, boy. Are you hurt?"

Randal stayed curled up on the ground and shook his head. Maybe his cousin would go away. But no . . . Lord Alyen and Sir Palamon had always taught that a true knight took the less fortunate under his protection, and Walter seemed intent on living up to the ideal.

"Let me look at you, boy. Is this blood on your face?"

Randal shook his head. "It doesn't matter, my lord," he muttered.

Then he realized that his cousin wasn't going to go away as long as he lay there on the packed dirt. He tried to stand, but the last kick to his knee had been too much for him, and he faltered as he came upright.

A strong arm caught him before he could fall. Randal felt the limber muscle beneath the heavy chain mail and a linen surcoat. Walter had grown over the last three years from a gangly boy into a young man of almost twenty. Randal looked away, still hoping not to be recognized.

11

"Here," said Walter. "Let me give you a hand."

He slipped an arm under Randal's and began helping the young wizard limp back toward the lighted inn. Randal muttered something he hoped sounded like thanks; his voice hadn't finished changing when he'd left Doun for the Schola, so maybe Walter wouldn't remember him well enough to recognize his voice and accent.

But Walter had never been stupid. He paused, and the idle kindness in his voice changed to genuine curiosity. "What's your name, boy?"

A wizard never tells anything but the truth, thought Randal, despairing. *Lies and magic don't work in the same mouth.*

"Well, answer me," Walter said, more sharply this time. "What's your name?"

"Randal," Randal said, almost in a whisper. Then, more strongly, "Randal of Doun—cousin."

II.

Squire

RANDAL SAT ON the floor of the small room that Walter had rented for the night. The young wizard dabbed at his cut cheek with a wet rag and looked up at his cousin.

"When did you get here, anyway?" Randal asked. He wrung out the rag into the wooden bowl on the floor in front of him, dampened the scrap of cloth with fresh water from the pottery jug beside the bowl, and dabbed at his cheek again.

"I came in after dark," Walter said. "They had to open the gates for me. I'd barely gotten done seeing to my horses when I heard that racket outside the stable."

Walter sat on the lumpy pallet that served as the room's only mattress, his long legs stretched out in front of him. The smoky light of the tallow candle cast flickering shadows across his face. As soon as he'd latched the door of the room behind Randal and himself, he'd stripped off his surcoat. Like the surcoats worn by most knights, Walter's outer garment was blazed with his heraldic device—the same design that he bore on his shield. Walter had chosen

14

a simple pattern of the family colors of red and gold, divided along a line from his right shoulder to his left hip, with a green pine tree in the forefront. After the surcoat, he removed his chain mail and his arming coat—the quilted tunic he wore underneath the mail. Now he was dressed in just a light linen undertunic, almost as stained by sweat and travel as Randal's was.

He's been on the road for quite a while, too, thought Randal, and Walter's next words confirmed his guess.

"I'm heading for Tattinham," said Walter. "I'll be fighting in the tourney there."

Randal wasn't surprised. Even before he left Doun to study wizardry, he'd known that Walter would be following the tournaments as soon as Lord Alyen would let him go. If Walter had remained at Doun until his father died, with no work of his own, he could only have grown restless and possibly troublesome. Sending him out to fight in the tournaments was dangerous, but in the long run kinder to everybody. Such a course wasn't uncommon— Randal himself might have done the same if he hadn't chosen the path to wizardry instead.

"Have you been on the road long?" Randal asked.

Walter nodded. "I was knighted last year. At first I traveled with Sir Palamon, but now I'm on my own."

He paused, and fixed Randal with a knowing gaze. "But what I'm doing here doesn't matter. The question, cousin, is what are *you* doing here?"

Randal dropped the damp rag back into the bowl and shrugged. "It's a long story."

"I didn't think it'd be a short one," said Walter dryly. "But I don't have anything else to do tonight. How long have you been living like this?"

"Working my way?" asked Randal. "Since spring. I was in Tarnsberg before that, studying wizardry."

"I suppose that traveling magician what's-his-name took you there."

"Wizard," corrected Randal. "Madoc's a wizard, not a magician. Yes, I left with Master Madoc."

"That's what Father said," Walter told him, smiling a little. "Sir Palamon and Sir Iohan—now, those two were in a rare fit. They were saddled and bridled and ready to ride after you. The man-at-arms who'd seen you go but hadn't stopped you was quaking at the look on their faces."

"Then what happened?" Randal asked.

"Not much," said Walter. "Father called Sir Palamon and Sir Iohan to him, and after he'd done talking with them, they sent their mounts back to the stable and never spoke of you again."

Madoc said he'd told Lord Alyen, Randal remembered. *It must have been an interesting conversation.*

But Walter's brief amusement had already died away. "You shouldn't have left without saying goodbye to me, at least. You know I wouldn't have told anyone."

Randal looked away from his cousin, and down at the bowl of water. "I didn't think you'd understand."

Walter didn't say anything. After a moment, a

16

knock on the door broke the uncomfortable silence. "That'll be the food," Walter said, sounding relieved at the interruption. "Are you hungry?"

Randal nodded. Walter went to the door and opened it. Outside lay a wooden platter with a meat pie and a loaf of bread. A leather bottle of water rested on the floor beside the platter.

Walter cut the pie in half with his dagger and handed a portion to Randal. The young wizard bit into the pastry and juicy beef, and felt thankful for the kitchen scraps he'd eaten earlier—without those to take the edge off his appetite, he'd have shamed himself before his cousin by tearing into his dinner like a hungry animal.

"So," said Walter, when all the food was gone. "Tell me about Tarnsberg."

Randal was silent for a moment. How could he describe the Schola to somebody who'd never studied there? Walter would never know an apprentice wizard's bitter frustration when a common charm refused to work, or understand the heady joy that came from seeing a difficult spell turn out right at last.

"It's a city on the western coast," said Randal finally, without looking up. "I studied magic there."

"For three years?" Walter asked.

Randal nodded. He could sense his cousin looking at him, and Walter's next question came as no surprise.

"Can you show me some?"

"You mean, do magic?"

"Yes."

17

Randal shook his head. "I can't."

"What do you mean, you can't? Didn't you learn anything in three years?"

"More than I wanted to," said Randal. "I'll tell you all about it someday, but not now."

He gave a quick, involuntary shudder. Just the memory of the last time he'd worked magic—in Master Laerg's demon-filled tower room, crowded with scaly horrors seeking to drink his blood—was enough to make his mouth go dry. He reached out for the leather bottle of water, and felt his wrist caught in Walter's muscular grip.

He didn't resist as his cousin turned the hand, palm upward. "That's quite a scar," said Walter, after a few seconds. "How did you get it?"

"I grabbed the wrong end of a sword."

Walter laughed. "Sure you did. After all of Sir Palamon's training! That's a good one, Randy . . . you grabbed the wrong end of a—"

Then Randal saw his cousin's amusement start to fade as Walter got a closer look at the red, slanting scar.

"You're not joking, are you?" said Walter quietly. "That's recent, too. Do you want to tell me about it?"

"No."

"Randal," said Walter, "whatever happened, you're still family. Is there somebody I'm going to have to kill for this?"

"No," said Randal again. He pulled his hand away and closed his fist to hide the scar. "He's already dead."

Walter gave him a long, considering look. "I see. And what about you? Are you going somewhere, or are you just drifting about?"

That, at least, Randal could answer. "I'm heading for Tattinham, and from there about a day's journey into the mountains. There's someone I have to find up there."

"That's wonderful!" Walter seemed genuinely pleased. "We can travel together for a few days."

Randal fingered the cut on his cheek and gave his cousin a doubtful glance. "Will you be going with those . . . with the others?"

"Why, yes, I suppose I will. Safety in numbers . . . oh, I see your problem." Walter frowned. "We'll have to tell them you're my squire. They'll never suspect you were the boy they beat up in the dark."

"Probably not," said Randal. *Besides,* he thought, *Reginald and all his friends put together probably aren't smart enough to make a guess like that.* "But I won't lie about myself," he told his cousin. "I'm a journeyman wizard; even if I can't work magic, a wizard doesn't speak anything but the truth."

"I'm not asking you to lie about anything," said Walter, a little stiffly. "After all, cousin, I'll be giving my word on this as well. You'll be wearing my colors, riding my spare horse, helping me arm and seeing to my needs—which means you'll be a squire in truth—if you haven't forgotten how."

"I remember," said Randal with a sigh.

"Fine," said Walter. He blew out the candle, leaving the room dark except for a scrap of moonlight slipping through a chink in the shutters. "Then good night, and wake me in the morning."

The rooster in the inn yard started crowing before the sun rose. Randal got up in the pale gray light of false dawn and dressed himself in his cousin's spare surcoat, and then awakened Walter just as the sun came up.

"Well, squire," said Walter as he belted on his sword, "we're off for the road." He smiled at Randal. "I tell you, it's good to have a familiar face beside me again."

"Let's hope it's not too familiar," said Randal. "Sir Reginald won't be pleased with you if he recognizes me."

"Leave Sir Reginald to me," said Walter. "Just do your work and stay out of his way."

But in spite of Randal's fears, none of the knights who gathered in the common room downstairs—Sir Philip, Sir Louis, or Sir Reginald—gave any sign of recognizing him. By daylight, the three looked ordinary enough, nothing like the shadowy figures who had knocked him about the night before. Sir Philip, the youngest of the three, had a look of reckless enthusiasm about him. *All action,* judged Randal, *and no thought.* Sir Louis was the oldest, round-faced and heavyset; by the time he reached middle age, he would be fat. Sir Reginald, who'd started the ugly sport, was the tallest and strongest. In a fair fight, Randal thought, he might come close to being a match for Walter.

None of the knights paid any attention to Randal's cut cheek or to the bruises along his jawbone. Instead, they greeted Walter and ignored Randal— a squire, like any servant, was just a part of the landscape.

All five members of the little party soon mounted and rode into the early morning. The sun shone out of a clear summer sky, drying the dew from the grass and from the damp brown dirt of the narrow road. In the foothills of the eastern mountains, however, the air never grew too warm for comfort. A cool breeze blew down from the high ground, ruffling the hair of the riders and making a stirring sound among the trees.

Randal hadn't ridden on horseback for over three years. He'd left Castle Doun on foot, and had traveled on foot ever since. He knew that he couldn't have handled the big, heavily muscled warhorse that his cousin Walter rode. Fortunately, Walter's other horse was a palfrey—a smaller, gentler-tempered animal, trained for endurance and smoothness of gait, not for going into battle. Randal found that what his mind had forgotten about good horsemanship learned in boyhood, his body remembered. He soon accustomed himself to the palfrey's ambling pace, and settled back to enjoy a pleasant morning's ride.

He told himself that the sun was bright, that his cousin's company was a welcome surprise, that by traveling on horseback he was certain to reach Balpesh—and his own magic—that much sooner.

After a while Walter dropped back from the company of the other three knights and rode beside him.

"You're awfully quiet this morning," Walter said after a few minutes. "Is something wrong? It's a beautiful day."

"I know," said Randal. "It's just—I can't explain."

Walter gave him a curious look. "You've been saying that a lot recently."

Randal shrugged. "Life's more complicated than I used to think it was."

"Something else you learned in Tarnsberg?"

The half-teasing question hit harder than Walter had probably intended. Randal thought of Laerg, who had looked like every apprentice's ideal of a master wizard, but who had nearly brought down the entire Schola with his wickedness.

He looked over at his cousin. "Yes," he said, without smiling. "You could say I learned it there."

Walter gave up trying to jolly him out of his bad humor after that. Shortly after noon, the party overtook a solitary knight also heading toward Tattinham. When they had drawn close enough to see the device emblazoned on the rider's shield, Walter spurred his warhorse forward with a shout.

"Hallo, Sir Guillaume!"

The other knight halted and turned toward the outcry. "Well met, Sir Walter!" he shouted.

He galloped back along the road to join the little group. There, Walter introduced the newcomer to the other knights.

"This is Sir Guillaume of Hernefeld, whom I think some of you already know by reputation. I've seen him fight, and have fought by his side, and can tell you that he is both valiant and courteous."

Sir Guillaume was a young knight, about Walter's age, with dark hair and a thick moustache. He bowed from the saddle to Sir Reginald and his companions. "It's good to meet friends on the road at last—I'd begun to fear that I was the only fellow going to a tournament in this forsaken region."

The day wore on. About midafternoon, the road began a long downhill slope toward a line of trees that snaked from horizon to horizon across their path.

"Lubac River," said Sir Reginald, pointing at a glimmer of water among the trees. By daylight, among friends of his own rank, the young knight seemed a pleasant fellow—but Randal hadn't forgotten the man's arrogant tone and hard fist in the dark of the inn yard. "I'm told there's a ford here," the knight continued, "and an inn about two hours beyond."

All the riders urged their horses forward, Randal along with the rest. The knights arrived in a group at the water's edge, where slender poplars grew along the riverbank, and a shallow spot in the river allowed men or carts to go across. Here at the ford, the river was broad and moved slowly, but Randal could hear the rushing noise of white water, and saw that a little farther downstream, the river broke into foam as it passed over unseen rocks.

Sir Philip urged his horse into the clear blue water to scout the way to the other side. The ford was shallow—the water didn't even dampen the knight's stirrups as he rode across. On the opposite bank he halted, looked at the ground, and then swung down from his horse to look closer. Then he stood, faced the others, and gestured for them to hurry.

The other knights put spurs to their horses, and came charging across the river. At the top of the bank, Walter called out, "What have you got, Sir Philip?"

"A rare mystery," the knight replied, "and a chance for some sport." He pointed at the road. "What do you make of those marks?"

Walter scanned the ground with a hunter's keen and experienced eye. Randal could remember him looking over the tracks of deer and wild boar in much the same way during their boyhood together at Castle Doun. "There was a fight here," he said. "Not more than a day ago. Three riders were attacked from both sides by men on foot."

The young knight pointed to where the grass at the sides of the road was broken and pressed down. "See, there's where the attackers lay in wait. And the tracks of the horses go this far along the road, and no farther—but there they are again, leading off into the woods."

Randal, listening, didn't doubt that Walter was right. The journeyman wizard remembered the merchants who'd ridden into the Basilisk from the direction of Cingestoun. The merchants had traveled on horseback, and a man-at-arms accompanied them to help guard the pack train. They'd left at dawn yesterday, heading for the market fair at

Tattinham—but it looked as if they hadn't gotten very far.

"So what do we do now?" asked Sir Reginald. "Ride on?"

"And turn our backs on a chance for fame and glory?" asked Sir Philip. "Of course not!"

Sir Guillaume was more practical. "How many of them are there?"

"No more than a dozen," said Walter. "And they're on foot."

"Well, let's go looking," said Sir Guillaume. "But not for too long. I'd hate to be caught in the woods after dark."

"If the next inn is no more than two hours down the road," said Walter, "we'll have time."

Guillaume nodded briskly. "Then let's go."

The little group of knights turned their horses' heads away from the road they had been following and rode into the forest to their left. The knights strapped their shields to their arms and drew their swords, riding forward as quietly as they could. The dark, sturdy oak trees surrounded them, and the branches arching overhead cast a deep shade, making the forest even cooler in the cool day.

Randal shivered a little. *I don't like this place*, he thought. He turned to his cousin. "Walter—"

"What is it?"

I can't explain. . . .

"Nothing," said Randal.

They rode on. Before long, Randal heard noises ahead: raucous shouts and laughter, the ringing note of an ax biting into a log, the crackling of a

25

bonfire. The knights were at the edge of a sizable encampment, but still they had not been noticed or challenged.

"Sounds like somebody's having a party," Sir Louis observed in a low voice. "Don't they believe in keeping watch?"

A few moments later, Randal understood the reason for the lack of sentries. Between the close-set tree trunks of the deep forest, he saw a clearing full of rough-looking men. Most of them were drinking from a huge cask that stood near the center of the camp. Some of the men had already fallen asleep on the leafy ground, and others sat singing and joking around a roaring fire.

Randal spotted three horses tethered on the far side of the clearing. Two stood in the shadows, but dappled sunlight shone on the third. He recognized it as belonging to one of the merchants who had left the Basilisk in the clear light of the previous dawn. The horses kept moving about uneasily, made nervous by something that hung from a tree nearby. At first Randal couldn't make out the details of the hanging object, but then it twisted in the wind and he saw the thing clearly.

It was the body of the merchants' guard.

III.

Night at the Inn

RANDAL TURNED HIS head aside and shut his eyes. Nearby, he heard Sir Guillaume remark, "That fellow must have given them some trouble," and Sir Reginald grunted in agreement.

Randal opened his eyes again. Now that he knew who to look for, he could see the merchants as well. The two men lay trussed up on the ground, stripped of their fine clothing and covered with dirt and blood. A large bandit squatted beside them, poking at them with a knife and watching them wiggle.

"Looks like a couple of captives there," Sir Guillaume went on. "Maybe we can get a reward by saving them."

Walter spoke for the first time since they'd seen the camp in the clearing. "Reward or no reward, I can't see any choice but to help them. Reginald, Louis, you two circle around on horseback and make sure none of the bandits try to flee." He paused, and then added as an afterthought, "Squire Randal, stay back and keep my palfrey out of the fighting—she's no warhorse, and might panic. Philip and Guillaume, charge when I give the word."

The young wizard felt his lack of magic keenly. He could imagine casting panic among the outlaws with a sudden fireball or a crash of thunder, and preventing loss of life on either side. Instead, he had to hang back in the shadows while faint rustlings and jinglings from the underbrush told him that Walter and the other knights were working their way into position.

Then Walter's deep voice shouted "Charge!" and the knights burst out of the forest into the clearing.

The outlaws sprang to their feet and grabbed their weapons. Most of them had short swords or pole arms, but a few had nothing more than knives and wooden clubs to use against the five armored and mounted men.

Sir Philip, still eager for sport and glory, was riding in the forefront of the charge. One of the outlaws swung a halberd at the knight, taking him in the side. He fell from his horse and went down in the press of men.

As Randal watched, his cousin Walter swung down from his horse and headed on foot toward the fallen man. The young knight strode forward toward where his companion had fallen, his shield held before him, his sword cocked at the ready behind his back. Sir Guillaume joined him, standing on Walter's left, the rims of their shields almost touching. Their long blades rose and fell as they cut their way toward Sir Philip.

The other two knights, Sir Reginald and Sir Louis, circled on horseback around the knot of bandits. The mounted knights fought with sword in one hand and shield in the other, guiding their horses with their knees. Whenever their blades flashed down, another of the bandits fell.

Sir Philip's riderless charger broke out of the turmoil in the clearing and headed for the forest. As the wild-eyed animal surged past Randal, the young wizard made a grab for the flying reins, caught them, and steadied the beast. Then he rode far enough forward to catch up with the abandoned horses of Walter and Sir Guillaume, and gathered the reins of all three chargers and the palfrey into his hands.

In spite of the danger, Randal found himself half-smiling as he restrained the skittish animals. *I can't fight,* he thought, *and I can't do magic, but I can at least manage to hold the horses.*

When he looked back at the clearing, no one except the knights was standing. All around the camp, bodies lay sprawled on the ground. Sir Reginald rode up to where Walter and Sir Louis knelt beside Sir Philip. "Stupid fools," Reginald said, with a gesture at the dead men. "They should have scattered and waited for us in the woods."

"It wouldn't have made any difference," said Sir Philip from the ground. "We'd have beaten them anyway." He coughed, and then rolled to the side. Walter and Sir Louis helped him get to his feet.

"Are you hurt?" Sir Louis asked.

"A bruise or two," Sir Philip replied. "Nothing worse." He bent over with his hands on his knees, breathing heavily. "My chain mail stopped most of it."

Sir Philip straightened, and then walked over to one of the bodies that lay sprawled on the ground nearby. He turned the body over with the toe of one boot. Randal recognized the outlaw who had been tormenting the merchants.

"He paid for his folly," was all the knight said.

Walter went to the two bound men on the ground, while the other knights began to search the camp. Randal stayed where he was on the edge of the clearing, still holding the horses.

Dead men littered the ground. Randal looked up toward the sky. Like everything else over the past few days, the small, brutal skirmish in the woods only served to bring home to Randal how wide the gap had grown between himself and the life he had once known—the life he had given up for his pursuit of magic.

Once he might have felt, like Sir Philip, that the outlaws had gotten what they deserved. But nothing was that simple anymore. Even from where he stood, holding the knights' horses, he could see that most of the dead men were shabbily clad, and many were gaunt from hunger. *They never had a chance,* he thought, *not against knights in armor.*

He shook his head. *If you'd come this way alone,* he reminded himself, *you'd probably be dead yourself by now. You aren't going to see Walter wasting tears on a gang of bandits.*

In fact, Walter was untying the captured merchants and offering them water. The two were in bad shape, but still alive—possibly the bandits had thought that they were worth some kind of ransom. Meanwhile, Sir Reginald and Sir Louis came up with a heavy chest between them.

"This is all the robbers had," Sir Reginald said. "Time to be going."

"No," said Walter. He gave a glance toward the hanging corpse of the merchants' guard. "There's one more thing we have to take care of first."

"We can't afford the time to dig a grave," said Sir Reginald. "Not if we want to reach the inn before dark."

"We can spare a moment for an honest man's last need," said Walter firmly, and Sir Reginald fell silent.

As it turned out, the grave was mostly dug by Randal, since the use of tools like shovels was beneath the station of knights when a squire was available for the work. After the burial, the knights set out again for the inn that Sir Reginald had heard was nearby.

By the time the group of knights reached the road, the sun had traveled more than halfway down to the horizon. Sir Reginald frowned at the western sky. "We'll be riding hard to reach the inn, thanks to you," he said to Walter. "There's no safety outside of walls in these parts."

Walter merely looked amused. "Then hard riding it shall be," he said. With that he urged his horse into a canter, and soon all the group, including the wounded merchants, were riding fast down the highway.

In spite of the pace Walter set, it was nearly night-fall by the time they reached the Headless Man, the inn on the Tattinham road that was their goal, and Sir Reginald was in a foul humor.

The group swept into the courtyard of the inn and dismounted. Sir Reginald flung the reins of his charger to Randal. "Make yourself useful," he said in a harsh tone. "Take care of the horses."

I've heard that speech before, thought Randal, but he said nothing as he led the high-spirited warhorse away to the stable.

Seeing to the animals' needs kept him occupied for some time. *At least we should have good company to-night,* he thought, *judging by the number of horses in the stalls.* Yet later, when the journeyman wizard entered the common room of the inn, he saw only one guest besides the group of knights and the two merchants they had freed from the bandits.

Strange, thought Randal, *for an inn this near a town to have so few guests. And where did all the horses come from?*

Still, the place seemed pleasant enough. A fire burned in the hearth, and the dinner was hot and plentiful; meat pies and roast pork, with cider and ale in abundance. The landlord, a fat, jolly man eager to please his noble-born guests, beamed cordially at everybody, including Randal, but the young wizard, for all that he had been close to starving the day before, found himself lacking in appetite. He sipped at a mug of hot cider, listened to Sir Philip and Sir Louis arguing about falconry, and thought about the puzzle presented by an inn with a full stable and so few guests.

After dinner the guests went upstairs to bed. The rooms were larger than the ones back at the Basilisk, had cots instead of pallets on the floor, and the paneling on the walls was of shiny, dark wood. Randal had lived over a carpenter's shop in Tarnsberg, and had learned enough about woodworking to know that the fine, polished wood was only a parchment-thin layer covering the cheap boards underneath.

There is always something hidden under the surface, he thought. *Isn't anything ever what it seems to be?*

Walter stretched out on one of the cots with a sigh of exhaustion. "We'll spend tonight in comfort, at least."

"I hope so," said Randal. He checked to make certain the door was shut, and then turned to face his cousin. "Walter, there's something funny about this place."

Walter looked at him. "What do you mean, 'funny'?"

Randal tried to put his suspicions into words. "Have you seen the stable? It's full, Walter—by the time I got through stabling our horses, there wasn't an empty stall left. So where are the other guests? We only saw one."

"Maybe he's a horse trader," said Walter. "They go to the market fairs, especially when there's a tourney in the offing."

"Maybe," said Randal. "But still . . ."

"If it makes you feel better," Walter said, "we can

take turns staying awake all night. I'll stand the first watch."

Randal lay down fully clothed, but sleep eluded him for a long time. He hadn't been aware that he'd drifted off until Walter was shaking him awake. "It's midnight. Your turn."

Randal got up and stretched.

"Take the watch until moonset," Walter told him, "then I'll take it to dawn. Do you want my sword?"

"No," said Randal. "I swore that I would never use a knightly weapon again, regardless of the need."

Even in the moonlight, Randal could see the disbelief on Walter's face.

"That was a stupid thing to do," said his cousin flatly.

"I didn't have a choice," Randal told him. "You can't be a wizard and fight with steel."

Walter shook his head. "I can't see that being a wizard's done you much good so far," he said. "Still, if you swore, there's no room for question. A man who breaks his word is nothing."

He lay down on the cot. "Wake me if there's trouble," he said, and closed his eyes. Soon he was snoring gently, with the long sword lying on the floor close to his hand.

The night wore on. A patch of moonlight came through a chink in the window. Randal watched it move across the floor and up onto the wall. *When it's gone,* he thought, *I can go back to sleep.*

But then, he heard something out in the passage: a metallic clink, like two keys knocking together. He would have thought nothing of it, except that it seemed to him that somebody stifled the noise.

Someone sneaking around? he wondered. *A thief, maybe?*

He went to the door and unlocked it, then opened it a crack. Outside, he saw nothing but blackness. He hesitated, wondering if he should wake his cousin, then stepped out into the hall. There, the darkness was so thick it could almost be felt. He turned to the right, and felt his way forward, keeping his hand on the wall.

He came to a door—the room where one of the merchants was staying—felt for the latch, and lifted it. *Not locked,* he thought. *Strange.*

He pushed the door ajar. The shutters were open, allowing moonlight to flood the room. After the dark of the hall, Randal blinked at the sudden brightness. He looked at the room. The man who slept there lay entirely too still. In the moonlight, Randal could see a strangling cord buried in his neck.

Randal turned and stumbled out of the room. The door to Sir Louis's room, directly across the hall, fell under his hand. Moonlight lit this room as well. But the sleeper did not stir. Blood ran from a huge gash on the knight's forehead.

Randal turned back into the hall, and rushed toward the room he had shared with Walter. The door to the room was open although Randal was sure he had closed it behind him. He dashed toward the room, and saw, through the door, the host of the

35

inn standing above the sleeping knight, a club in his upraised hand.

"Walter!" Randal shouted.

The club came down. At the last moment, Walter rolled aside—and the club smashed into the pillow where his head had lain. Walter rolled to his feet with three feet of naked steel protruding from his right fist. Randal had never seen anyone draw a blade that fast.

The man with the club turned to face the knight, and again the bludgeon smashed down. Walter blocked the blow with his sword, and then swung. The man crumpled.

Randal turned in time to see another man coming up behind him, lunging with a knife. The young wizard sidestepped, and caught the arm as it came past him. He pulled the man forward into the room, where Walter waited.

"They're killing everyone!" Randal shouted. "Bandits!"

Walter pushed past his squire into the hall. He went up one side of the passageway and down the other, pounding on the doors with the pommel of his sword.

"Up and arm!" he shouted. "Outlaws are upon us!"

It was only too true. Armed men were coming up the stairs at each end of the passageway—at least a dozen of them—some with knives, some with swords, some with clubs. One or two on each side carried lighted torches.

By the flickering red light, Randal saw that the

36

surge of men would soon overcome Walter. *Magic,* whispered the voice of temptation in his ear. *A spell, or we're all dead.* Just as firmly, he pushed the idea away. *Walter is right. If I break my word, I'm nothing.*

Randal's cousin thrust with the point of his sword, and a man in the front rank of the bandits fell, knocking into one of the torchbearers behind him. The brand, knocked from the second man's hand, fell to the floor, where it rolled up against the thin paneling of the inside wall.

But Walter was getting pushed back, step by step. In the narrow confines of the hall, he couldn't fight with the great swinging arcs that a broadsword required. He was thrusting with the point of the blade, and blocking with the edge, but Randal knew that he would soon be surrounded.

Just then, the door across the hall from Randal's room swung open. Sir Reginald looked out, still wearing his nightshirt, but with his sword in hand. "What in the name of thunder—" he began.

Then he saw the press of men crowding up the stairs and into the hall. Without hesitation, he stepped out of the doorway and took his place behind Walter.

Together, the two of them were better off, but still the situation was desperate. Then Sir Philip was there, sword bared. The third knight had taken the time to slip his mail coat over his head before joining the fray. Now the three young knights were able to push back against their attackers.

Randal heard a loud crackling sound starting to rise above the noise of the combat. Flames from the fallen torch had licked up the tinder-dry wood of the paneling, and had run into the thatched roof above. A red light played over the mass of fighting men, and acrid smoke billowed forth from the burning thatch.

Then, in the midst of the smoke and glare, the outlaws made a final charge. The weight of their bodies pushed back the knights, and Randal was crushed against the wall. He fell, and felt another body fall on top of him. Squirming out from under the dead weight, he crawled to the nearest open door.

He stood inside the room, coughing in the smoke, then made his way to the open window. He climbed out, and hung by his hands above the dirt of the courtyard. Then he dropped.

Rolling, he came to his feet and looked around him. Sparks from the burning roof scattered across the sky. Some had fallen on the roof of the stable, and the building was already starting to burn.

The horses . . . thought Randal, and dashed for the stable, dodging from shadow to shadow as he ran. He opened the stable door and ran inside, then stopped. Red flames licked at the bottom of the roof, and the horses were bucking and neighing in terror. Randal knew that their plunging hooves could kill a man in an eyeblink—but without horses, the knights would never get as far as Tattinham even if they did win free of the inn.

Better kicked in the head than burned or butchered, Randal told himself. He opened the stalls and drove out the maddened beasts, flattening himself against the

stable wall as they thundered past. *Now for the saddles.*

He forced himself farther inside the burning building. The knights' gear was still where he had put it earlier; he located it mostly by feel in the thick smoke and lugged it over, piece by piece, to the nearest window. Then he started heaving it out into the yard.

The air in the stable grew hotter as he worked. Smoke filled his lungs, and he had to pause from time to time to cough and gasp for breath. Finally, Randal tossed the last piece of tack out the window onto the ground, and clambered after it.

Seconds later, the stable roof collapsed behind him with a tremendous roar.

IV.

Tattinham

RANDAL SCRAMBLED TO his feet and started dragging the saddles and other gear beyond the reach of the flames. Out in the inn yard, the black night had turned red with the light from the twin fires of inn and barn. Shadowy figures of outlaws passed in front of the doors and lower windows of the Headless Man, illuminated by the flames. Panicky horses swirled and plunged around the yard. Then out of the inn's main door came four men close together, standing in stark outline against the orange fire that shone from the burning building.

From where he stood in the shadows, Randal saw that the four knights were still in danger of being overpowered. He looked at the yard full of horses. As he'd expected, the knights' chargers could be easily picked out from the rest by their size and quality, and by their lack of fear now that they were out of the burning stable. The noise and the smell of fighting, by themselves, had little power to frighten creatures bred and trained for war.

Just the same, Randal thought, as he struggled to put saddle and bridle on his cousin's charger, *I wish*

I could use a calming spell right now. I don't need to get my ribs kicked in this close to finding Master Balpesh and getting my magic back.

One by one, he saddled and bridled the other horses. Over by the door of the burning inn, the four knights were still fighting. Gathering up the reins of the warhorses, Randal swung onto his palfrey. Right through the band of outlaws he rode, sending them dodging in all directions as the great horses threatened to trample them into the dirt of the yard.

"Mount up!" he shouted over the noise of the fighting. "Mount up!"

Walter looked around and up at the sound of Randal's voice. "Well done!" the knight exclaimed, mounting his charger as he spoke. "I feared you were dead in the fighting upstairs."

Randal had no time to answer. The other knights had mounted their horses as well, and now they turned as a group and charged the outlaws still remaining in the yard.

Against men on foot, a knight on horseback was close to invincible. Even though they were not completely armed or armored, the four knights scattered the men before them. Soon the gray light of dawn came through the smoke, and revealed Walter and his companions to be the sole possessors of the field.

"Nothing left here," Sir Philip said, poking at the charred rubble of the inn. "And no sign of Louis."

"He's dead," said Randal. "The innkeeper killed him—or the bandits did."

"Not much difference between the two," said Sir Philip. The young knight looked at the ruins of inn and stable. "Well, at least Louis has been avenged."

"Not that it's doing him any good," Sir Reginald snapped. "Or us, either. We lost everything but our skins in that fire."

"Not quite," said Walter. "We have our horses, thanks to my squire, and whatever else was left with them in the stable."

Sir Guillaume strode up in time to overhear Sir Reginald's complaint. He looked pleased with himself in spite of the situation. "And thanks to me, we have our armor—I had a chance to toss all of it out the upstairs windows. We may smell of smoke for a few days, but we can still fight at Tattinham."

"Then we don't have anything to worry about," said Walter. "Whatever else is lost, we can replace with the help of our winnings."

The four knights put on their armor, and then rode out into the pale dawn, leaving behind most of their finery—and a good deal of their money as well—in the ashes of the inn.

The next day, they reached Tattinham just as the sun was setting. Tattinham was a walled town, not as large as Tarnsberg, the port city on the western sea where Randal had attended the School of Wizardry, but certainly several times larger than Doun, the village below the castle where Randal and Walter had spent their younger days.

The tourney field itself lay outside the walls of the town. There the companions went their separate ways amid the scores of tents and pavilions put up by the knights fighting in the next day's tournament. Walter's pavilion had been in the stable of the Headless Man, along with his saddle and other gear; it smelled heavily of smoke, as Sir Guillaume had predicted, but otherwise had come to no harm.

Like a good squire, Randal set up the pavilion and started a small campfire. Sir Guillaume, meanwhile, set up his own tent near the spot Walter had chosen. Sir Reginald and Sir Philip had gone to camp elsewhere, at which Randal was quietly pleased—the loss of their friend Sir Louis had not sweetened Reginald's temper, and if he ever did connect Walter's squire with the stableboy back at the Basilisk, he might decide to challenge Walter then and there.

Night was settling fast over the campground. Lanterns and torches and dozens of cooking fires sparkled star-like on the hillside. From somewhere far off, Randal could hear a ballad being sung, its melody drifting over the sounds of men and horses preparing for the night.

Feeling weary but content, he began to cook supper for himself and his cousin. Walter, meanwhile, had stripped off his surcoat and armor. He sat beside Randal at the fire, wearing only his quilted arming coat, whetstone in hand, and his bare sword across his knees.

Then Walter's horses snorted. Walter was on his feet in an instant, facing out into the night with his sword ready before him. In the dark, nearby, an unseen hand stroked a chord on a lute, and an alto voice sang:

"O I could have married the king's third son,
And he would have married me,
But I forsook a crown of gold
And it's all for the sake of thee."

Randal felt a thrill of recognition. *I know that voice,*
he thought. *But I never expected to hear it so far from
Tarnsberg.* "Lys!" he called. "Is that you?"

"Me and no other," said the voice, and the lute
player stepped forward into the circle of firelight.

In spite of her name, the newcomer wore a boy's
tunic and hose. Her disguise had never fooled Randal, and didn't seem to be fooling Walter, either—
the young knight had lowered his sword and was sit-
ting down again with an amused expression. The
slim, slightly built girl could well be taken for a boy
by the unobservant, which gave her a small amount
of protection on the dangerous roads of Brecelande.

She gave Randal a quick hug, and then stepped
back. "I'm glad to see you made it this far in one
piece," she said. "What happened to your face?"

"Nothing serious," said Randal. "And it's good
to see you, too—but what in the world are you doing
here? The last time I saw you, it looked like you were
planning to stay in Tarnsberg until the sea rose and
the mountains fell."

"What am I doing here?" echoed Lys. She sat
down cross-legged on the ground beside the campfire. "I'm looking for you, that's what I'm doing—
and I gave up a good job singing for my supper at

the Gryphon Tavern in Tarnsberg to do it, too, so you'd better be grateful."

Randal looked at her suspiciously. "This wasn't Master Madoc's idea, was it?"

"As a matter of fact," said Lys, "it was."

She plucked at the strings of the lute, a lingering chord that hung in the night air like a question. "It was strange, too . . . he came into the Gryphon a day or so after you'd left, and told me to pack up and come along. He wouldn't say why, either—just that I had to meet you here before you started up into the mountains." She shook her head at the memory. "We traveled fast, let me tell you. My feet are still sore—and I thought I was used to life on the road!"

"Is Madoc here in camp now?" Randal asked hopefully. It had been over four months since he'd last seen the master wizard who'd given him his first glimpse of the wonders of magic.

"No," Lys said. "I've been in town for a month already, waiting for you. He headed on north."

Randal's spirits fell. "Oh, well," he said after a moment. "He's not the sort to stay in one place very long. I wonder, sometimes, how he managed to stick around Tarnsberg long enough to make it through his apprenticeship."

All this while, Walter had been listening to the conversation with a look of mild amusement. Now he spoke for the first time. "Aren't you going to introduce the fair damsel?"

Randal felt his cheeks redden. "This is Lys," he said. "She is of Occitania, and a true friend." He paused, and added, "I owe my life to her friendship."

Walter rose and bowed. "Then I'm in your debt as well, Demoiselle Lys, since Randal is my cousin. I'm Sir Walter of Doun." The knight sat down again, and said, "A friend of Randal's from Tarnsberg, are you? Can you do magic?"

"No magic," Lys replied. "But a little of everything else. I've been everything from actress to acrobat in my time, though mostly I make my way with song."

Walter turned to Randal, and said, laughing, "I think all Tarnsberg folk must be half-mad. I find you, heir to a barony, wandering the land and mucking out stables to earn your keep—and now here's a lady of the Southlands, singing for hers."

Walter went back to sharpening his sword. Without looking up from his task, he asked, "Will you be attending the tourney tomorrow, Demoiselle Lys?"

"I don't know," she said. She glanced over at Randal. "How long are you staying in Tattinham?"

"I'm here as my cousin's squire," he told her. "I can't leave until the fighting's over."

"Then I'll be staying as well," she said. She stood and slung the lute by its strap over her shoulder. "But I have to leave you for now—there's an inn full of travelers in Tattinham who've been promised music with their supper."

After she'd left, Walter looked across the campfire at Randal. "A gallant damsel."

"Yes," said Randal. "She is."

Walter looked at him a second longer in silence, and then said, "She knows what happened in Tarnsberg, doesn't she?"

Randal dropped his gaze to the little tongues of red flame running through the coals of the campfire. He remembered Master Laerg's tower room at the Schola, and the demon that had tried to lap up the blood running from his sword-slashed hand. If Lys hadn't brought Master Madoc to his aid, the demons would have taken him, blood and all.

"She knows," he said to Walter. "She was there."

His cousin put aside the whetstone he'd been using, and looked down the blade of his sword, turning the blade this way and that to check for nicks and dull spots. The newly sharpened edges gleamed in the firelight.

"If she knows all about it," Walter said at last, "can't you trust me with at least a part of the story?"

Randal sighed. His cousin had helped him without pressing for more information than he was willing to give—he supposed he did owe Walter the rest of the tale. "I was at the Schola in Tarnsberg," he began. "Learning magic. I wasn't very good at first, but I scraped through the classes and found a master wizard who took me on as his apprentice."

"Madoc again?" asked Walter.

"No," said Randal. "I wish it had been . . . the master who taught me was a man called Laerg. He was good at his work—I learned a lot from him, and I learned it fast. But it turned out that Laerg had plans of his own. He wanted to take control of the

48

kingdom, and he'd bargained with demons for the power to do it."

Randal paused and poked at the fire with a splinter of wood before going on. "Laerg had promised the demons the blood of a wizard in return for their help. My blood, as it turned out."

"You look like you've still got most of it," observed Walter. "Is that when you cut your hand?"

"Yes," said Randal. "He had a sword. Not for a weapon—whatever he was planning to do, he was too much of a wizard for that—but as a magical symbol of the spell he was working to call the demon princes and control them. But I killed him with it, instead."

Walter looked pleased. "Good for you, cousin."

"The Regents of the Schola didn't agree with you," said Randal, with a crooked smile. "As a wizard, even an apprentice, I'd forsworn the use of any knightly weapon. So the Regents patted me on the back with one hand and slapped me hard with the other. First they passed me out of my apprenticeship and made me a journeyman wizard, and then they made me swear not to use any magic at all until I got permission."

"If that's why you've been sleeping in stables and letting yourself get beaten up by the likes of Sir Reginald," Walter told him, "then I say you ought to swallow your pride and come home until those Regents of yours lift the ban."

"It's not like that," Randal said. "I can't just wait around. I have to find a particular wizard—his name's Balpesh, and he lives in the mountains close to here—and ask his leave to do magic again."

Walter snorted. "And if you get yourself killed wandering around without either sword or spell to protect you, is it not their fault? A fine set of people, these Regents, if you ask me."

The two cousins finished their supper in silence, put out the cookfire, and went into the pavilion. Walter rolled himself in his blankets and soon began to snore. Randal, for his part, lay awake a while longer, wondering why Master Madoc had wanted Lys to meet him in Tattinham. He fell asleep, still mulling over the possibilities . . . and dreamed, and knew that he was dreaming.

He dreamed that he awoke and found the pavilion empty, his cousin's pallet folded up and his clothes and armor missing. Judging by the daylight outside the pavilion, the hour was almost mid-morning; the tourney would be starting soon. Already, Randal could hear the high, yelping notes of trumpets and hunting horns summoning the combatants to the field.

I overslept, he thought in the dream. *Walter is going to kill me if I don't find him before the fighting starts.*

He dressed, pulling on the surcoat he wore as his cousin's squire, and hurried out into the camp. Like the pavilion, the camp seemed strangely empty. A cold breeze stirred the banners and sent the walls of the pavilions billowing in and out, but Randal saw no human movement anywhere. And no sound came from the camp except for the sighing of the wind.

Once again, the horns sounded from the direction of the tourney field.

Everybody must be over there already, thought Randal, and started toward the noise.

When he reached the field, he saw that the tourney had almost begun. Knights in armor strode about making last-minute checks and adjustments to weapons and armor, taking practice swings at the air to loosen muscles stiffened by sleep, arguing with squires and grooms about the state of their horses. Ladies in elegant gowns clustered under an awning on one side of the field. Servants of all sorts, wearing the colors of a score or more different knights and noblemen, ran about on a multitude of errands. Heralds in bright tabards consulted their scrolls, conferred with each other in loud voices, and consulted their scrolls again.

And all of them—knight and lady, highborn and lowborn—were animals, though they walked like men. Here a man took off his helmet and revealed the muzzle and fangs of a gray wolf; there, a lady turned in Randal's direction, and he saw the pointed, vicious face of a weasel framed in her linen wimple.

I don't like this, thought Randal.

"Walter!" he called aloud. He began looking about for his cousin's pine-tree shield. "Walter!" he cried again.

Then, through the crowd, he spotted his cousin's tall, armored form. Lys was with him, dressed as Randal had never seen her, in the gown of a fine lady. To Randal's relief, they both still had their

51

own faces, though neither Walter nor Lys appeared to notice that the knight with whom they were speaking had the bristly snout and small, angry eyes of a wild boar.

"Walter! Lys!"

Randal shouted the names as loudly as he could, and started running across the tourney field toward his cousin and the girl. But neither one seemed to hear him; instead, they nodded civilly at the boar-knight and moved away deeper into the crowd of beasts, out of Randal's sight.

He ran after them, threading his way through the throng in the direction they had gone. Always, they stayed just out of reach, never giving him more than a glimpse of Walter's ginger hair or Lys's cap of black curls before vanishing again. He called out to his friends again and again, but the voices of the beast-men drowned his cries, and his ears were full of their harsh, growling babble.

Then, suddenly, a high, human scream cut through the air, and the crowd before him parted. It was Lys who had screamed; the lute player stood motionless as a statue, and Randal's cousin lay beaten and bleeding at her feet.

V.

Blood Sports

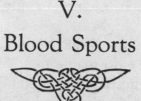

RANDAL CAME AWAKE with the sound of his own outcry echoing in his ears.

Walter rolled to his feet, grasping his sword. He looked alertly around him.

Early sunlight filtered through the material of the tent and shed a pale gray light over his features. For a moment, Randal seemed to see his cousin still covered with blood; then the last traces of the nightmare faded.

Seeing no threat, Walter focused on Randal's face. "What in the name of heaven and earth are you yelling about?"

Randal drew a deep breath. "I had a dream."

"Well, have a quieter one next time, will you?"

"I'm not joking, Walter. I had a dream. This tourney . . . there's something wrong here. I saw it."

Walter looked at Randal with a puzzled expression. "You saw what?"

"Trouble," said Randal. "Deceit. They were all animals. . . ."

"What in the world are you babbling about?"

Randal clenched his fists. His scarred hand ached in the cold morning air. He forced himself to speak slowly, in measured tones. "I'm talking about the future, Walter. It comes to me sometimes, in dreams."

"Hold on a minute," said Walter, frowning. "You said you couldn't do magic now."

"This isn't something I do," Randal told him wearily. "It's something that happens to me whether I want it or not. This time—don't fight today, Walter. Something bad is going to happen. I know it."

"*How* do you know it, Randy? You never used to go in for prophecies back at Doun."

"I hadn't spent three years at the Schola then, either," said Randal. "And I tell you, I saw you lying dead, or the next thing to it. Don't go out on the field today—please."

Walter shook his head. "A fine fool I'll look, won't I, when the heralds announce that I'm not fighting because my squire had a bad dream."

Randal looked at his cousin for a moment in silence. He couldn't tell whether Walter believed him or not. But the stubborn expression on the young knight's face made it clear that further argument was useless.

"Marshal's call!" came a voice from outside the pavilion. "Marshal's call in one hour! All those who will fight today must gather on the field in one hour!"

The herald moved to another part of the camp, repeating his message as he went. Walter wrapped his quilted arming coat around him. "Help me, will you? I don't have much time."

Silently, Randal assisted his cousin with his armor. Walter strapped on his sword and picked up his helm and shield. He left the pavilion and strode in the direction of the tourney field. Randal watched him go.

I tried, thought the young wizard. But the words gave him no comfort.

After a while, he left the now-empty camp and made his way down to the field. The day was warm, and the bright sunlight glittered off the steel of the knights' armor and weapons. Banners and surcoats made vivid splashes of color between the blue sky overhead and the green turf underfoot.

Randal looked about, half expecting to see the animal faces from his dream. His cousin was nowhere in sight; instead, he found Lys standing on the sidelines of the field near the spot where Walter had planted his banner. A cold shiver went through Randal at the sight—she wore the same blue gown that she'd worn in his dream.

He saw her start to frown as he approached. "What's wrong?" she asked as soon as he came within earshot. "You look dreadful this morning."

"I had a dream," he said.

Lys paled a little at his words. Her reaction didn't surprise him. The lute player remembered the last time such a dream had come to him. He had nearly died, and Master Laerg had nearly destroyed the School of Wizardry. So now she wet her lips and asked in a low voice, "What did you see?"

He told her. She looked around, as if expecting the men and women standing near them to turn to beasts on the spot, and then said, "What about your cousin? Didn't you warn him?"

"Of course I warned him," said Randal. "But do you have any idea how stubborn Walter is? I might as well have been talking to myself."

"So what are you going to do?"

Randal shrugged. "Without my magic, what *can* I do except hope that this time I'm wrong?"

As he spoke, a cavalcade of mounted men thundered onto the field, armed and armored, their banners waving.

A herald addressed the new arrivals. "Duke Thibault, are you and your vassals fighting today?"

"Not today," said the leader of the group. "We've come to watch the sport, nothing more."

"I don't like this," said Randal, under his breath. "I don't know what's wrong, but I don't like it."

"Neither do I," said Lys, "especially after what you just told me. Wait, what's that happening?"

Two knights had gone into a marked-off section of the field, and started cutting and slashing at one another with broadswords.

"They're beginning the tourney with single combats," said Randal. "Those two will fight until one of them yields."

Lys frowned. "Fight about what?"

"Nothing in particular, most of the time," a voice cut in before Randal could answer. Sir Guillaume, wearing his armor but not his shield and helmet, strolled over to join the two younger people. The knight went on, "Sometimes one man or the other will have a real grievance. But usually they just fight for the practice or for the honor of winning."

Even as Guillaume finished speaking, another voice carried to them across the field, loud and confident. "I challenge you, Sir Walter of Doun!"

"Oh, no," said Randal. "Not Sir Reginald."

Guillaume looked puzzled. "What's wrong with him?"

Randal chose his words carefully. "He beat a stableboy a couple of nights ago, and Walter made him stop. He's probably still nursing a grudge."

As Randal watched, Walter and Sir Reginald went out onto the field. The marshal cried out, "My lords, do honor to the duke our patron," and the two knights flourished their swords toward the castle that rose in the distance above the trees.

"Time was," said Sir Guillaume, "that marshals in Brecelande would begin a bout by calling for honor to the King."

"Do you remember those days?" asked Lys. No king had ruled in Brecelande since the High King had died and his infant daughter had vanished years before.

"Oh, no." Guillaume laughed. "Do I look that old? I heard the tale from my father."

The marshal cried out, "Do honor to your noble opponent."

The two knights saluted each other by striking their swords against their shields with a ringing blow.

"Then for honor and glory, lay on!" the marshal cried.

For a moment, neither man moved. Then Randal, watching, heard Lys gasp as Walter slipped his shield off his left arm and tossed it away onto the grass.

"Nice," murmured Sir Guillaume in an appreciative tone as Walter gripped his sword in both hands, with the blade held at the vertical in front of him. "Very nice."

"I don't understand," said Lys. "Why did he throw away the shield?"

"He's using the sword two-handed, like a greatsword," said Sir Guillaume. "That puts more strength into his blows, and allows him to attack from more directions. But it's risky—the blade has to be both sword and shield at once—and only a man confident of his own skill would choose to fight that way in a challenge bout."

Sir Guillaume sounded admiring, but the knight's words only served to renew Randal's feelings of coming doom. *Walter's fighting like that to show the whole world what he thinks of Sir Reginald,* the young wizard realized. *If the stableboy Reginald was roughing up hadn't been me, Walter might have just fought him sword-and-shield and been content. But no, he's decided to rub it in. . . .*

Out on the field, the two knights circled, keeping their distance. Then Reginald stepped forward and cut at Walter's helmet with an overhead blow.

"It's all a matter of style," Sir Guillaume explained further. His eyes were intent on the field.

"Walter carries a hand-and-a-half sword—it's longer and heavier than Sir Reginald's broadsword, but not so long and heavy that it can't also be used one-handed by someone strong enough."

"And is he?" asked Lys. "Strong enough, I mean."

Randal thought back to the fight against the bandits and how Walter had swung that sword with one hand, the long blade arcing through the air in a steely blur.

"Yes," he said. "Walter is strong enough."

Meanwhile, Walter had blocked Reginald's first blow easily, but the attack had been nothing more than a feint. Now Reginald's blade dropped and became a cut aimed at Walter's rib cage. But Randal's cousin pushed his own blade over and down to block the blow. The swords met, singing, and then sprung apart.

Walter swung into a shield-side attack on Reginald's leg. Reginald pivoted his shield downward and blocked, but Walter used the speed of the rebound to come around in a blinding half-circle toward Reginald's helm on the sword side. Reginald stepped back and blocked with his own blade, but the superior length and weight of Walter's sword told against him. The strength of the two-handed blow forced the other blade downward to ring against Sir Reginald's helm.

Reginald opened his shield away from his body to punch the metal rim against Walter's armored chest. But Walter pivoted with the swinging shield, and swung his blade with all the strength in his shoulders, twisting his body to add the power of his hips to the edge of his sword.

The blow took Sir Reginald in the back of the helm as he stepped forward. Reginald stumbled, his lunge turning into a fall, and lay face down on the field.

Still holding his sword with his left hand, Walter reached down, pulled on Sir Reginald's shoulder, and turned him onto his back. Then he placed the point of his sword at the eye slit in Sir Reginald's helm.

"Yield you, sir knight."

Sir Reginald's gauntleted hand relaxed, letting go of the hilt of his sword. "I yield."

Sir Walter helped Sir Reginald to his feet. Then the two men walked to the colored ribbon that marked the edge of the field, ducked under, and vanished amid the other knights, leaving the heralds to mark down the results of the bout.

"That's it?" Lys asked, in disbelief.

"It's more than you seem to think," Sir Guillaume answered. "Sir Walter now owns Reginald's arms and armor. If Reginald wants them after today, he'll have to buy them back."

A short while later, Walter came over to join Randal and the others. The young knight carried his helmet in the crook of his left arm. Sweat ran down from his hair and left streaks in the dust on his face.

"Water," he said hoarsely to Randal. "That was hot work out there."

Randal hurried to fill a goblet from one of the barrels of drinking water set up around the edges of

the field. As he handed the goblet to his cousin, he muttered, "Have you fought enough now?"

"No," said Walter. He drained the goblet and held it out again. "I'm having a good time, and I'm doing well. How else am I going to get the practice that I need to fight well in war when it comes?"

"If it comes, you mean."

Walter shook his head. "When."

The heralds began to cry the arming for the grand melee, when all the knights at the tourney would take part in a mock battle. Walter drank one final goblet of water, then mounted his horse and rode away to join the others. This time he took his shield.

The afternoon wore on. Shouts and sounds of passages-at-arms came across the field, and sometimes two knights would fight within sight, but for Randal and Lys, alone now that Sir Guillaume was fighting among the rest, the afternoon went slowly.

From time to time, one knight or another would escort a prisoner back from the field. Walter appeared once, bringing a prisoner with him, and Randal asked him how it was going.

"Fair enough," Walter replied. "I've captured this one, and two others. When they ransom their horses and armor, I'll be able to replace everything I lost in the fire."

Suddenly, Randal noticed movement among the spectators on the field—Duke Thibault's troop was mounting. "I've changed my mind," the duke called to the chief marshal as he and his men spurred their horses onto the field. "We tourney today!"

"That's not fair!" protested Lys. "His troop is

fresh, and everybody else has been fighting since this morning.''

"Who said anything was supposed to be fair?" asked Randal bitterly. "I was right. This tourney *is* full of animals.''

"I could have told you that," Walter responded with a brief laugh. "I've seen them before. Nothing that I haven't handled before, either.''

Randal's cousin turned his horse and rode back into the melee. Not long after, Sir Guillaume came out of the press, followed by Duke Thibault. The young knight had been captured; he took off his helm and chain mail and waited with the other prisoners in the safety zone at the end of the field.

Then, as the day grew older, Walter reappeared, leading another man's horse by the reins. His captive was easily recognized: Duke Thibault himself.

Randal watched as Walter galloped the duke and himself over the plain, fending off rescue attempts by the duke's men along the way. Randal could see that Walter had the duke's sword tucked into his own belt. Walter swung down from his horse, as did the duke. A crowd of knights pressed around them.

Several men shouted at once, and the crowd surged back. Randal started forward, knowing with a cold certainty that he was going to see his cousin Walter lying still on the ground. As in his dream, but far worse—the blood welled out of the back of Walter's right shoulder, painting his surcoat a dark and ugly red.

I tried to warn him, thought Randal. Already he was

running across the field, with Lys close behind him. *I tried . . . what am I going to do now?*

"What happened?" he demanded as he sank down to his knees beside his cousin and struggled to remove Walter's helm.

"Somebody hit him from behind with a mace."

Randal recognized the voice of Sir Guillaume. Without bothering to look around, he asked, "Did you see who did this?"

"No. Just the mace." Sir Guillaume paused a moment. "But I saw Sir Reginald nearby when it happened."

Randal lifted his cousin's heavy steel helm free and laid it aside. Walter's face looked gray and clammy, and his lips were blue.

"We need a healer," Randal said. "Lys—?"

"I'll find one," she promised, and ran off.

Randal sat back on his heels and looked about for help in carrying his cousin back to his pavilion. Duke Thibault was nowhere in sight—it appeared that Walter's noble prisoner had used the confusion to disappear without paying the ransom for his horse and armor. Randal's lips tightened. *I have half a mind to track him down and ask for it myself,* he thought. *But with the shape Walter's in, I can't afford the time.*

Randal turned and glanced up at Sir Guillaume. The young knight appeared pale and anxious.

"Help me get him back to the pavilion," Randal said. "If we can get him up on a shield . . ."

Working together, the knight and the young wizard wrestled a shield under Walter's unconscious body. They carried him back to the pavilion he and

Randal shared. There they began, slowly and carefully, to remove his armor. The heavy coat of chain mail was the hardest—it covered Walter from neck to knees, and threatened to press his breath out with its weight. At last it came off, and Randal saw that the garment underneath it was drenched with blood.

At least he's still breathing, thought Randal. The young wizard didn't want to think about what might lie under the blood-soaked clothing. The blow had come from a mace, Sir Guillaume had said, and a mace was an ugly weapon: a spiked metal club that crushed flesh and splintered the bone beneath.

Randal was still trying to work up enough courage to peel away the quilted tunic when the healwife arrived. Lys entered the pavilion close behind her.

"I came back as fast as I could," said Lys in a breathless voice. "Mother Shipton is the best healwife in town. I found her tending the day's cuts and bruises, and convinced her we had something more serious here."

The healwife was already kneeling beside Walter. "You shouldn't have moved him," she told Randal and Guillaume. "A fragment of bone could puncture his lung, or cut a blood vessel inside, and then no skill on earth could cure him."

But despite her words, she began to examine the wounded man, pulling the quilted tunic away from his shoulder the better to see the injury. Randal looked down at the ground, feeling ill, and then forced himself to look back again; behind him, Sir Guillaume turned away.

The healwife looked at Randal. "Get me some water," she said, "and some light. Then leave, so that I can weave my spells in peace."

Randal obeyed. Then, with Lys and Sir Guillaume, he waited outside the pavilion for the healwife to be done with her work. Night had fallen by the time Mother Shipton emerged from the tent, and when she did, her shoulders sagged and her footsteps sounded weary.

Randal wet his lips. "Well?"

"I've done the best I could," she said. "But I doubt that he'll thank me for it."

Randal felt himself grow cold. "Why not? What's wrong?"

"Whoever struck him has a powerful arm," said the healwife. "The shoulder blade is shattered beyond my ability to mend."

"Will he die?" asked Lys.

The healwife gave a tired shrug. "Don't let him move for six weeks, and he'll heal as much as he ever will. All the pieces of bone are in place—that much, at least, I was able to do. But it would take a master wizard to make that shoulder work again."

VI.

Into the Mountains

STILL SHAKING HER head, the healwife walked away. Randal, Guillaume, and Lys re-entered the pavilion. Walter lay on his stomach, the injured arm bound to his side with strips of cloth. A single candle-lantern gave enough light for Randal to see that his cousin was awake.

Walter's hazel eyes, dull now with pain, focused on Randal. "I should have listened to you."

Randal couldn't think of anything to say. Instead, it was Lys who spoke—and to Randal, not Walter.

"You studied at the Schola, Randal—*do* something."

Sir Guillaume looked startled. "What's this? A wizard?"

Randal ignored him. "You know I can't," he said to Lys. "And even if I could, what the healwife said is true. Curing a wound like this would require the services of a master wizard, and not just any master at that."

"Well, then," said Lys. "You're going to be seeing a master wizard, aren't you?"

Randal laughed without humor. "I'm hardly in a position to ask Balpesh for any favors."

"You're not," said Walter slowly. "But there's nothing to stop me from asking on my own."

"You need to stay here and finish healing," Randal told his cousin. "Mother Shipton said—"

"I'm not deaf," said Walter. "I heard what she said. I'm going with you."

Randal thought of the mountain path to Balpesh's tower as Master Madoc had described it to him at the Schola, and shook his head. "Horses can't go where I'm going."

"Then I'll walk." Walter's face was set in lines of pain, but his voice was firm. More quietly, he added, "You wouldn't want to leave me alone among the wild beasts, would you? Whoever wanted me down wanted me dead."

Randal couldn't argue with him. Sir Guillaume asked quietly, "Did you see who struck you?"

"No," said Walter. "Just a sort of blur. I got my head out of the way, but my shoulder wasn't so lucky." He closed his eyes for a moment, then opened them again and looked at Guillaume. "Take my armor and horses, and hold them for me. If I don't come back, they're yours."

Throughout the night, either Randal or Lys stayed awake by Walter's side. They brought him water to drink, and eased him into more comfortable positions. In the graying morning, Randal wrapped a long cloak around his cousin's body, over the blood-caked arming coat. Together, Lys and

Randal helped Walter put his boots on, and then, at his insistence, strapped his sword around his hips.

"A knight is never without his sword," Walter said, more to himself than to anyone. Then he stood. He swayed, caught himself, and stood straighter.

The three walked out of the sleeping camp. Low fog, mixed with smoke from the campfires, shrouded the ground. Most of the combatants at the tourney had been to a feast the night before, and the camp slept deeply. Without a sound, the three friends were away.

Before the morning was half gone, Randal felt certain that bringing Walter along had been a bad mistake. As long as the way remained clear, Walter was able to match the slow pace Randal set, although the wounded knight's face was pale, and his mouth set hard.

But a little before mid-morning, the way to Balpesh's tower split off from the main road to follow the course of a swift-flowing stream that ran down the mountains. Randal followed the directions Madoc had given him at the Schola, traveling parallel to the watercourse on a narrow path that led uphill along the bottom of a deep ravine forested with birch and aspen.

Their pace slowed as the path climbed upward, and Walter grew still more pale and tight-lipped. But they made steady progress, nonetheless, until they rounded a bend in the path and saw a rockfall blocking the way. The pile of dirt and boulders stretched from the steep slope on their right to the white water rushing by on their left, covering the path completely.

They halted. Walter sank to the ground and leaned with his good shoulder against the support of the rock face. His eyes were closed, and Randal could hear his long, shaking breaths. Lys stood over him with her hands on her hips, and looked from Randal to Walter and back again.

"Now what?" she asked. "We can't climb that pile of boulders—not with one of us already hurt."

Randal shook his head and considered Lys for a moment. Once again, the young entertainer had worn the boy's clothing she preferred for traveling, and carried her lute slung over her shoulder in a leather case. Of the three of them, he had to admit, she knew the most about life on the road—if she said the rockslide couldn't be climbed, it couldn't.

"Then we have to clear the way," he said. "Walter, lend me your sword for a few minutes."

His cousin's eyes snapped open. "You're not going to use my blade for a crowbar!"

"No," said Randal. "I'm going to use it for an ax. One of those saplings will make a good lever if I can cut it down."

"An ax," said Walter. He shook his head. "There's wizardry for you—making a knight's weapon into a woodcutter's tool."

Randal drew a deep breath. "There are a dozen magical ways to get across that rockfall," he said, "from levitating us over it to summoning an earth elemental to throwing all those rocks to the other side of the stream. As it is, I have to do this the hard way. Will you please give me the sword?''

He paused and saw with a touch of shame that Walter was already trying to draw the heavy blade left-handed.

"Sorry," Randal muttered as he took the offered weapon. The scar on his palm ached as he curled his hand into a tighter grip. The blade was heavy—far heavier than he'd expected—but just grasping the hilt brought memories. He could see the rich velvet of Master Laerg's ceremonial robe, smell the pungent reek of incense, and hear the frightful echo of the chant that opened the gate to the demonic plane.

Thrusting the images aside, he strode over to one of the saplings near the water's edge and swung the sword against the tree's slender trunk.

The shock of the blow made his hand sting, and he heard Walter's voice from behind him. "It'll work better if you use both hands."

Randal put his left hand around the bottom of the sword's hilt, and swung again with all his force. A chip flew from the tree. He ignored the ache in his right hand, the sweat rolling down his back under his tunic—everything—as he cut again and again into the growing notch.

Soon the small tree fell to the ground, and Randal stripped off the branches. Then he and Lys together began to lever rocks off the path and into the stream.

As they worked, they talked. "Are you sure this is the right road?" Lys asked. "I'd hate to do all this work and then find out we were going the wrong way."

"It matches the directions I got back at the Schola," said Randal. "But this rockslide . . . how long do you think it's been here?"

They put their weight onto the lever, and more stones rolled off the pile and down into the water.

"It looks recent to me," said Lys.

Randal nodded. "That's what I thought."

"Do you think it means anything?" Lys asked.

"Everything means something," Randal answered. "The trick is figuring out what."

He straightened and looked about. Rubble still covered the path, but the newly made gap revealed the way continuing on the far side. Where the rock-fall had been, a smaller pile of loose rock, uneven but passable, remained. At least their efforts had opened a way that could be scrambled over, rather than climbed.

"That's as good as it's going to get," Randal said. "Let's go."

He helped Walter to his feet, and then aided him in resheathing the sword. Randal and Lys took up positions on either side of the wounded knight to brace him over the uncertain ground, and all three strode through the newly cleared gap. The going was slow, with smaller rocks shifting under their feet as they crossed the loose heap of stones and dirt, but nobody stumbled or fell.

Then they were past the rockfall and walking more easily. Randal looked at his cousin. Walter's face was ash-colored under the tan and dirt.

"Can you go on?" Randal asked.

Walter nodded, but Randal saw with a chill of foreboding that his eyes were fever bright. Small beads of perspiration stood out on Walter's forehead, and the young knight's jaw was set, as if he held back a cry of pain by strength of will alone.

The path continued upward. Soon it turned away from the stream, and cut sharply uphill to the right, making one switchback after another as it climbed up the side of a steep cliff. On one side of the path, the cliffs towered up to the sky; on the other, the rock fell away in a sheer drop to the stream below.

As the trail climbed upward, it broke into a series of carved stairs. Randal remembered the stairs from the directions he'd been given; Balpesh's hermitage wasn't far away. Even now, he thought that he could see a stone tower in the distance ahead, framed in a gap between two mountain peaks.

But is it close enough? he wondered. Walter was lurching from side to side with each step, and Lys had moved to support him with a shoulder under his left arm. And the air was growing chilly. Even though it was only mid-afternoon, the tall peaks cut off much of the sun, and the breeze coming down the snow-capped mountains made Randal shiver. Walter never complained, but Randal knew the cold wind had to be cutting through him without mercy.

"Let's take a rest," Randal said. "We could all use one."

Lys gave him a quick, grateful glance, and helped Walter lower himself to the ground. Then she came forward to join Randal. "Are we going to make it to that tower before dark?" she asked in an undertone.

"We're close," Randal told her. "But if I remember right, we have to cross the stream first."

"How?"

"There should be a bridge," he said. "Up where the gorge starts to narrow again."

"I hope you're right," Lys said. She glanced over where Walter sat huddled inside his cloak, then turned back to Randal with a grave expression. "Because I don't think your cousin can last through a night out in the open."

They went on climbing the cliff path step by painful step. Then, abruptly, they turned a corner, and saw that the path continued on the far side of the stream.

The two paths were connected by pieces of what had once been a stone bridge. The central span had collapsed, leaving a gap of some thirty feet between the broken ends still standing. A tall, lightning-struck fir tree stood beside the bridge on the far bank of the ravine. Nothing stood on the near side but a broken stump.

"That's it," Walter said. "We're stopped."

Randal looked down. Two thousand feet below, the threadlike current tumbled in white water over sharp rocks. He dropped a stone. It vanished from sight as it fell, and he never saw a splash nor heard a sound. He looked back at the wreckage of the bridge.

"No," he said. "That dead tree is taller than the

gap is wide. If we can get it down, we'll have our bridge."

"In case you hadn't noticed," Lys pointed out, "the tree is on the wrong side."

"I know," said Randal. "I'll have to jump across."

Lys shook her head. "Wrong," she said. *"I'll* jump."

Randal stared at her. "You?"

"Me," she said. She looked pale and frightened, but her eyes were serious. "I'm lighter, and I've worked as an acrobat. If you jump and miss, it'll all be over. No magic, no healing, nothing. If I miss . . . what's another lute player, more or less?"

She unslung her lute and thrust it into Randal's hands. "Here, hold this."

Without further discussion, she went off the path, past the ruined bridge, heading for the place where the gap between the two cliffs was narrowest. She clung to the rock face at places to do it, but she soon reached a point where nothing separated the cliffs except five yards of empty air.

"She'll never make it," muttered Walter.

"Yes, she will," said Randal. *I hope,* he added to himself. Lys was surefooted and stronger than she looked, but the jump was longer than any he himself had ever tried, with a long drop to the water and stone below.

Biting his lip, he looked again at the shattered remnants of the bridge. The edge of the broken stone showed unweathered rock and fresh dirt on the line of the break. The wood of the broken tree stump to his right was fresh and white. He shook

75

his head. This bridge hadn't failed more than three days earlier; probably at the same time as the rock-slide on the trail behind them.

A shiver, brought on not just by the wind, moved up his spine. He was getting a bad feeling about what he might find if they ever reached the wizard's tower.

He turned away from the bridge and saw that up ahead, Lys had arrived at the narrowest part of the gap. She waved at him, then curled into a ball and flung herself over the empty space.

She missed the path by inches. Randal watched helplessly as she scrabbled at the loose rock with her outstretched hands. *I should have tried the jump myself,* he thought. *No matter what she said.*

Her fingers caught a small ledge just before the cliff turned vertical, and she came to a halt amid dust and rolling stones. Pulling herself up inch by inch, she got a foot into a crack and began to crawl up the steep slope. At last she threw a leg over the edge of the carved path, rolled to the top, and lay full length on the ground for a moment. Then she stood, and ran down the path to the far end of the bridge.

She pushed against the lightning-struck tree. It swayed a little. "The roots aren't deep," she called. "I'm going to push it over."

Lys put her back to it, and began rocking the dead tree in place. With a crackle and a crash, it toppled over. With its top branches caught on the cliff where Randal and Walter waited, it stuck, its base narrowly wedged among the rocks on Lys's side.

"There's our bridge," Randal said. "Let's go."

Randal helped Walter to his feet. They walked to the tree. Walter looked at the makeshift bridge and shook his head.

"This may not hold," he said. "I'll cross first. If the tree breaks with you on it, I'm likely to die before I can get back to Tattinham alone. If it breaks when I'm on it, I'll only go a little sooner. And better I should die than you anyway."

Randal started to protest, and then stopped. If Balpesh couldn't—or wouldn't—heal Walter, the young knight would never be able to use a sword again. *No wonder he's taking such chances,* Randal thought. *He doesn't really care whether this journey kills him or not.*

In silence, Randal watched as Walter made his slow, painful way across the gap. Unable to use his arms to balance himself, the young knight stepped carefully around the protruding branches, while the ends of the tree shifted and worked against the stones on either side. The wind blowing up from the gorge fluttered the bottom of his arming coat, and blew his hair across his face. He reached the far end and collapsed against Lys. Gently, she helped him sit again.

Randal slung Lys's lute across his own shoulder and stepped out onto the tree. He could feel it vibrate under him, and hear the the rocks grating under the branches. The cold wind flowed past him. He looked down once, then hurriedly fixed his gaze on the far bank.

Even as Randal reached the far side, the tree

began to wobble. The roots pulled all the way out of the earth with a snapping sound, and the trunk fell into the gorge. Randal sat down hard, and didn't dare look to follow its progress.

"That's it, then," said Lys. "No going back."

From this side of the bridge, the way to Balpesh's tower was smooth and easy. The path led away from the edge of the cliff and became a steep set of steps carved into the rock. The three reached the rise at the top of the stairs, and found themselves looking down at a small pocket of fertile ground set in the midst of the harsh mountain landscape.

A stream flowed through the valley, past a wattle-fenced farmyard containing a barn and a henhouse and a vegetable garden. In the center of the farmyard, a stone tower stood out stark black against the gray-and-white mountain that rose behind it. Even now, the sun was dropping behind that peak, and long purple shadows lay across the little valley.

"Well, here we are," Randal said.

And not a moment too soon, he added silently. Walter was swaying where he stood. Randal and Lys exchanged glances, and moved to support him on either side.

They walked down the gentle slope toward the fence. A simple gate, designed to keep animals in, rather than people out, blocked the path. Randal opened it and stepped through. He looked around the farmyard, and saw a pair of nanny goats, their udders heavy, waiting on their milking stands and bleating unhappily. In the pigsty, a sow rooted in an empty slop trough.

I don't like the looks of this, Randal thought. *But this is Balpesh's tower, all right. It has to be.*

His uneasiness grew as they walked up the flagstone path toward the front door of the tower. The tower's windows were shuttered, and the door was closed. No latch showed on the outside. Randal pounded on the door with his fist.

"Hello!" he shouted. "Open the door!"

Nobody answered. Lys helped Walter sit down, and then picked up a stone beside the path. She pounded on the door with the stone, and added her voice to Randal's.

Randal looked at her hands. They were red with blood. "Why didn't you tell me you hurt yourself climbing that rock back there?"

"She didn't," came Walter's faint voice from behind them. "The blood is mine. The wound opened again when I crossed the bridge."

Randal and Lys hammered on the door with even greater force. "Balpesh!" Randal shouted. "Let us in! We have a wounded man here! Help us!"

Only the echoes answered from the cold and empty hills.

VII.
The Tower

"NOW WHAT?" asked Lys.

Randal shook his head. "I don't know. Stay here, and I'll take a look around."

He set out to explore the farmyard. First he circled the base of the tower, but found no other doors and no windows lower than what would be the second level inside. He looked into all the outbuildings and again found nothing.

Nothing I can put a name to, he told himself. But three years at the School of Wizardry had strengthened in him senses that most people never used. Long before he finished his survey of the little farm, his skin had risen in gooseflesh, and the hair bristled on the back of his neck.

Something magical is going on here. I can feel it.

He came back around to the tower door, and saw Walter half lying on the threshold, leaning with his good shoulder against the closed door.

A few feet away, Lys prowled up and down the flagstone path like a nervous cat. She jerked around at the sound of his footsteps. "Oh, it's you," she said. "Did you find anything?"

"Nothing," he said. "There's no way in except hat door."

Walter gave a faint laugh. "I suppose a battering ram is out of the question."

Randal looked at him. "Take it from me, cousin, you don't break down a master wizard's front door and expect him to think kind thoughts about you afterward. And besides, this place has more spells on it than a dog has fleas."

"Spells or no spells," said Lys, "if we don't get inside before dark, we'll be sleeping in the barn with the goats. Unless you prefer the chicken coop."

Her voice was light, but Randal didn't miss the meaningful glance she sent in Walter's direction.

We have to get him inside, Randal thought. *The outbuildings aren't going to be warm enough once the sun goes down and the night wind starts blowing.*

"I've slept in enough stables on my way here," Randal said. "But I draw the line at goats and chickens. If you know a way to get in, I'm all for it."

"There's a proverb in Occitania," said Lys. " 'If the door's locked, try a window.' Give me a boost up to the top of the door, and I'll see what I can do about those shutters."

Randal made a stirrup with his clasped hands; Lys stepped into it, and he lifted her upward. The lute player put her fingers on the top of the lintel above the door and pulled herself up. She balanced sideways on the lintel, then swung herself over to a crack between two stones in the tower wall. From there, she worked her way up to the nearest window, and balanced precariously on the narrow sill.

"I think I can lift the shutters out of place," she called down to Randal.

"Do it," he told her, "and let's not think about what spells Balpesh might have cast on them."

But nothing untoward happened as Lys worked the shutters free and dropped them to the ground.

The window opening revealed was tall and narrow, and so small that even the slender lute player had to turn sidewise to wiggle through. Once through, she vanished. For long moments, there was no sound from the tower. Then the front door grated open, and Lys stood in the gap.

"Come on in," she said.

They went in. The first floor of the tower was clearly reserved for storage, though now it stood empty except for a few barrels and a couple of chests. A well opened in the center of the floor, and a bucket hung suspended from a rope over it. A circular stairway led up to the next level.

On the floor above, they came to a large, high-ceilinged kitchen with a generous fireplace. One window stood open, showing where Lys had gained her entry. A high-backed bench stood near the fireplace; Walter sank down onto it.

"It's dark in here," he muttered, "and cold."

The young knight was shivering inside his thick woolen cloak, and his teeth chattered. Randal and Lys exchanged glances. Then Lys moved quickly to throw open more of the kitchen shutters, and Randal knelt in front of the hearth. The fire had burned down to white ashes. Randal touched them.

"It's out," he murmured. "This hasn't been lit for days."

Lys came away from the windows. "Look at the table," she said, and pointed. "Whatever happened, it came suddenly."

Randal looked, and saw that the kitchen table had been laid for a meal—but the food had congealed untouched on the plates. Again, the cold finger of warning stroked down his spine. *This place is thick with magic,* he thought. *Serious magic, not just the guards every wizard puts up as a matter of course.*

"Let's get a fire going," he said. "And look for blankets."

He took some firewood from a pile next to the fireplace, and laid the sticks on the hearthstone. As he did so, he noticed without surprise that the iron pot hanging above the fire had boiled dry, and the contents had burned thick in the bottom of the vessel.

He took out his tinderbox and struck a spark to ignite the kindling. "Being the slowest apprentice at the Schola had its advantages," he commented to Walter as he fed slivers of wood to the flame. "It was two years, at least, before I had enough power to light so much as a candle. In the meantime, I got good at doing it the hard way."

By the time he had a blaze going, Lys returned with an armload of bedding. She and Randal made a pallet for Walter in front of the fire, and helped him to lie down. Randal flinched at the sight of the fresh blood, dark and slick, along the right side of

Walter's already blood-encrusted arming coat, but he said nothing.

Walter knew he was courting death when he started out this morning, the young wizard thought. *There's nothing you can tell him that he doesn't already know.*

He covered his cousin with one of the blankets Lys had brought. "Did you find any candles?" he asked her. "We may need some later."

"There aren't any downstairs," she said. "That's as far as I looked. I don't mind telling you, Randal, this place makes me jumpy."

"I'm not surprised," said Randal, with a crooked smile. "But we're going to need light before long."

He stood up from where he'd been kneeling in front of the hearth, and brushed the dust off his knees. "Why don't you keep an eye on the fire for a while? I have to search this place anyway, so I might as well look for candles while I'm doing it."

Lys didn't say anything for a moment. Then she shook her head and drew the small eating knife she carried in a sheath at her belt. "If you're going to be poking around upstairs," she said, "then I'm coming with you. You may be forbidden to use weapons, but I'm not."

Then Walter spoke from where he lay on the pallet by the fire. "Neither am I. And this place is too quiet for my liking. Cousin, could you put my sword by my left hand?"

Randal did as Walter asked, without comment, even though he doubted that the wounded knight had enough strength left to even lift the blade, let alone fight with it. Then Randal and Lys set out to explore the tower.

First they went downstairs to the storage room below and barred the tower door from the inside. Then they headed back up the spiral staircase, bypassing the kitchen and climbing as far up as they could. It was dark there, in the center of the tower, and Randal went by feel most of the way. At the top, he found the end of the staircase by hitting his head against the ceiling above.

He backed down a few steps and felt for a door. Finding one, he pushed it open. By the faint light that came from around the edges of a shuttered window, Randal saw a small room containing a bed and a small trunk. The bed hadn't been slept in. Randal opened the window, and found himself looking down at the farmstead from a considerable height.

"Nothing here," he said to Lys. "Let's work our way down."

They made their way back down the stairway, checking each room as they came to it. In one of the rooms, Randal found what appeared to be the wizard's study. A tall bookcase stood against the outer wall, between two windows. A magic circle, a small one, covered a portion of the floor. Burned out candles, set around the circle, marked the four main directions. A wooden box filled with still more candles lay on the table, holding open a book written in thin, spidery handwriting.

"Light for the night," said Lys. She reached out a hand, and then paused. "Is it safe to touch them?"

Randal shrugged. "Without casting a spell myself, I can't be sure." He dipped into the box and took out a double handful. "There's no enchantment on them that I can feel, anyway."

He paused for a second, his hand halting in midair above the wooden box. The handwriting in the book beneath was in the language of Brecelande, not in the Old Tongue that wizards used for most of their spells and scholarly writings. *It is worse than I thought,* read the first line, before the words disappeared under the box of candles. *We must take immediate . . .*

The box obscured the rest, except for part of another line at the bottom of the right-hand page. *. . . here. But time does not remain to call together . . .*

Lys spoke from close to Randal's side. "Have you found something?"

"Maybe," he said. "I'll come back and read it later. But first we have to check out the other rooms."

By the time Randal and Lys returned to the kitchen, night had fallen outside the tower. They lit one of the candles, and made a plain but filling supper out of sausage and hard cheese from the pantry shelf. Randal brought Walter's share over to him, but the wounded knight only shook his head weakly.

"I'm sorry, Randal, I don't think I could get it down."

"Don't worry about it," said Randal. He put a hand on Walter's forehead as he spoke; the skin felt cold and clammy to his touch. "Just rest. I have to go back upstairs and see to something."

Randal took two candles from Lys, lit one from

86

the fire, and headed back upstairs to the workroom. The few lines he had read in the open book had convinced him that the volume held a key to the mysteries of Balpesh's tower. Inside the workroom, he plunked the candle down onto the desk in a puddle of wax, moved the empty candle box to one side, and began reading the book from the beginning.

As he had suspected, the book was Master Balpesh's magical journal. The first half of the book dealt with magical researches so advanced that Randal hardly understood what they were about. Interspersed with the magical records he found accounts of the farm and similar mundane things.

Sometime during his reading, a light rain started outside. The wind blew clouds across the sky, blotting out the stars. The wind veered and set the candle flame wavering. Randal stood, closed the shutter, then sat and continued to read.

Then, toward the middle of the book, a line jolted Randal awake. *A great heaviness fills me. Trouble is brewing at the Schola. I can feel it, but all attempts at scrying are blocked, and the future is confused. I see a tree growing in the library of Tarnsberg, but what fruit it bears, I cannot guess.*

Again the ghostly fingers raised the hair on the back of Randal's neck. The date of the entry was the same as the day that Laerg had taken Randal as his apprentice—the day when Laerg's magic had aided Randal in creating a tree in the library of the Schola; the day when Randal had first begun to use his magical abilities to their full extent.

Randal read on. *My choice was correct,* said an entry

from six months before. *The unpromising apprentice that Master Madoc presented has borne out my predictions. Now he has been barred from wizardry as punishment for daring to wield a sword.*

Randal put his head in his hands. *Then there's no hope,* he thought. *Balpesh knows everything, and I was condemned before I even set out.*

From the sound, the rain seemed to be pouring down outside. Randal could hear it lashing at the closed shutters of the room. A feeling of despair swept over him. Suddenly, reading further seemed useless.

He stood up and walked back downstairs, taking the candle with him. When he entered the kitchen, he found Lys singing, her clear alto voice floating over the silvery ripple of the lute strings:

"If you will forsake your house-carpenter
And come along with me,
I'll take you to where the grass grows green
On the banks of the deep north sea."

She broke off the song as he entered, and turned an eager face in his direction. "What have you found?"

He sat down heavily on the chair by the kitchen table. "That we don't have a chance," he said, "and we never did have one. Balpesh already knows what happened back at Tarnsberg. And he agrees with the Regents that I should be banned from wizardry. We came all this way for nothing."

For a while, a deep silence filled the kitchen. Outside, the wind gusted around the tower. Somewhere in another room, one of the opened shutters banged against the wall.

"Maybe you're wrong," said Lys. "You can't give up now." In the candlelit darkness she made a small, fragile-looking figure, holding a lute almost as big as herself. Randal had to remind himself that without any magic of her own, she had once dared a room full of demons to help pull him to safety.

"Not now," she repeated, and Randal said nothing.

Far above, the wind wailed across the chimney of the tower, and the noise echoed down into the kitchen with a sound that resembled words, or the voices of a crowd of men. The fire on the hearth burned low; the draft down the chimney had pushed it down to a pale blue flame.

Randal shivered with sudden cold. He could see his breath in the chill air. "Magic," he whispered.

"Magic," whispered back another voice out of the dark.

Randal twisted to look in the direction of the sound. That side of the room was empty. Out of the corner of his eye Randal could see his cousin Walter lying on his pallet by the hearth. The long sword that lay beside the wounded man's left hand glowed with a pale blue light of its own.

Reflections, Randal thought, without conviction.

He looked at the hearth: the fire was almost out. Then smoke billowed up. Sparks and flames made an elongated, wavering face—eyes, a nose, an open mouth. Then the mouth moved, and spoke.

"Find me."

Lightning crackled around the tower, and thunder boomed so loud that it seemed to shake the stones themselves. In the ringing of his ears Randal thought he heard the door below—the one he himself had bolted shut—open and slam closed again. Then came the sound of footsteps mounting the stairs.

Randal looked over at Lys. The lute player, her eyes wide with fear, had risen to face the spiral stairway leading down into darkness. As Randal watched, she flung up one hand in a warding gesture. The words she called out were only a child's simple charm against nightmares, but they seemed to echo through the stone-walled room. "Unless you come in the name of the powers of light, then in the name of the powers of light, be gone!"

The footsteps stopped.

Abruptly, Walter sat up. His eyes snapped open and stared before him. He raised his arm and pointed at Randal. "Help me," he said.

The voice wasn't his cousin's. And the arm with which Walter had gestured was his right arm, the one with the shattered shoulder blade. The one that couldn't move.

"Randal," Lys hissed in a desperate whisper, "is this real?"

Randal nodded, his face pale.

As quickly as Walter had sat up, he lay back, his eyes closed again. Randal's throat had gone dry. He filled a cup with water from the pitcher on the table, and drank. After the first swallow, he threw the cup

away from him onto the floor, and spat the fluid out of his mouth—it was not cold, sweet water, but something thick, warm, and salty. Something like blood.

Dark liquid from the cup ran out across the floor, and as it ran it seemed to form a word in a shaky script: *Read.*

"What should I read?" Randal cried aloud.

But he already knew the answer. Slowly and reluctantly, he picked up his candle again, and started up the spiral stairs. As he climbed, drafts from nowhere plucked at his candle flame. The storm outside increased in fury.

Something has awakened, Randal thought. *Someone knows that I'm here.*

He sat at the master wizard's desk and returned to reading the journal. He read of how his old teacher, Master Laerg, had opened the gate to the demonic plane in an attempt to gain power by killing all the wizards in the world. But now Randal understood that the plan had not all been of Laerg's own making: the first idea had come from the demonic plane, in order to bring one of the demon princes into the world under no control except its own.

Several of the entries in Balpesh's journal discussed this possibility. At one time the wizard would dismiss the idea as unlikely at best, and at another would give new evidence in its favor. Then, in an entry dated only three days before, the journal stated positively, *There is no doubt. The demon Eram has escaped from the demonic plane, and now walks abroad in our world. It must be found and returned to its own place before it does true damage.*

Randal turned the page. The entry continued. *The situation is worse than I thought. We must take immediate action. I had hoped to gather the most powerful of the master wizards to aid me in the task, but this threat will not wait. Eram hopes to bring others of its kind across the void between worlds, and then the time for cures will be past. I must find a way to draw the demon to me, and then fight it myself. Surprise will be my only advantage. Anything other than swift victory will be defeat. I wish that I could bring even one other wizard here, but time does not remain for one to come. I alone will construct a trap in my secret workroom, and await Eram there. The day after tomorrow I believe the demon will come, but I must begin my preparations tonight.*

There were no further entries.

Randal closed the journal and stood up. The candle on the table was guttering out in a puddle of wax, and the storm had eased somewhat. A watery gray dawn outlined the shutters in the study windows. Slowly, he went back down the stairs and into the kitchen. Lys had been dozing on the bench by the fire; she sat up with a jerk as he came in.

"Balpesh is somewhere in this tower," Randal said, without waiting for her to speak, "and a demon is with him."

VIII.
Searches

"BALPESH IS IN his workroom, and I have to find him," Randal said. He sank down on a stool next to the kitchen hearth. "The room upstairs where we found the candles is just a sort of library. Balpesh did his reading there, and it's where he stored his books and papers, but I don't think he ever used it for anything more than minor magic."

Lys shook her head. She had dark circles under her eyes, like smudges of ink on her pale face. Looking at her, Randal felt renewed awareness of his own exhaustion. *It's been two nights since either one of us had any sleep,* he thought.

"We went all through this place," Lys said. "And we didn't find any workroom." A sudden gust of wind, stronger than the rest, rattled the kitchen shutters as she spoke.

"There's one hidden in the tower somewhere," Randal insisted. "There has to be. And Balpesh must be trapped inside." Randal sank down onto the bench next to Lys and rested his head in his hands. "I don't know what to do."

"Randal," said Lys quietly, "that business of your

not doing magic. That's just a rule, isn't it? Last time you broke the rules, it was for a greater good. Couldn't you break the rules for a greater good again?"

He looked up. "And use magic to find the hidden room?"

She nodded.

Randal sighed. "I gave my sworn word. If I break that, then I'm no wizard, and I've proved it out of my own mouth. When you're dealing with wizardry, stepping off the path even a little gets you hurt. I learned. Every time I clench my fist, I'm reminded."

Lys looked at Randal's right hand. Slowly he opened his fist and turned his hand palm up, showing her the puckered red scar where he had cut himself to the bone, saving himself from Laerg's spells.

"So what do we do?" she asked at last.

Randal pushed himself to his feet. "We find the secret room. Let's start tapping on walls."

The morning passed in fruitless tappings and trampings, while the storm raged outside. By noon, both Randal and Lys were exhausted, and the secret workroom, if indeed there was one, still remained hidden.

On the pallet by the hearth, Walter slept—but not the quiet sleep of healing. Instead, he alternately shook with chills and burned with fever, at one time kicking off his blankets, and at another shivering uncontrollably. Walter's eyes were deeply sunk in hollows, and his face appeared pale and waxy. Randal or Lys gave him water to drink whenever he awakened and complained of thirst, but they both knew that the young knight was slipping away in spite of their efforts.

About noon, Lys put the cup of water back onto the table beside the pitcher. "This isn't working," she said to Randal. "We've got to get something better than water into him."

Randal leaned his aching forehead against the stone wall. "We haven't got anything," he said. "Except for stale bread, dry cheese, and tough sausage. And I don't think I can take another meal of those myself."

"There's fresh milk and eggs outside," said Lys. "I can go out—"

Randal shook his head. "Not by yourself in a storm like that. I'll go with you."

"You need to keep looking for that hidden room."

"We'll only be gone a little while," he told her. "And maybe the wind and rain will clear my head a little. Besides, this is for Walter."

They put on their cloaks and made ready to go outside. Randal crossed over to where Walter lay by the hearth, and went down on one knee beside the pallet. His cousin's eyelids slowly lifted, and the hazel eyes focused on Randal.

"Randal?"

"It's me," Randal reassured him.

"Good," murmured Walter. "I've had some strange dreams. . . . Have you found your wizard yet?"

"Not yet," said Randal. "But I'm looking. Right now, Lys and I are going outside to get you something better to eat. Just rest easy until we come back."

Together, Randal and Lys went downstairs into the storeroom. Randal unbolted the massive, iron-bound oak door on the ground floor, and put his shoulder against it. He could hear the wind howling outside. He swung the door open, and the two stepped outside. They stepped into a sunlit garden under a blue sky dotted with high, fluffy clouds.

Lys gasped.

"Illusion," said Randal quietly. "Something is playing with our minds."

"Yes," said Lys, in the same careful tone. "But which is the illusion—the sunshine, or the storm?"

Randal shrugged. "Without magic, who can tell? But we came out to do something. Let's get it done."

They collected the eggs and milked the goats as quickly as they could. As they worked, the sunlit day took on a brittle stillness. The silence of the air made the sounds of birds and insects seem even louder. Randal was glad when the work was finished and he could return with Lys to the tower.

As soon as they stepped over the tower threshold, the storm resumed outside with full force. Randal closed the door against the raging wind, and slid the heavy bar into place. Then he and Lys went up the stairs and into the kitchen.

Randal carried the bucket of goat's milk over to the kitchen table. "We're back, Walter," he called out, as he reached for the cup and started to fill it.

"We'll have something better than dry cheese for you in a minute."

There was a moment of silence, and then Lys said, in a tight voice, "Randal. Walter isn't here."

Carefully, Randal set the cup of milk down on the table, and turned toward the hearth. Lys had spoken the truth: Walter's pallet was empty, and the long sword no longer lay on the floor beside it.

"He was feverish," said Lys. "Maybe he wandered off."

"Maybe," said Randal. A feeling of guilt swept over him for leaving his cousin. He didn't want to think about what else might have happened to somebody left alone and unwatched in the stronghold of a master wizard. Especially not after what they had seen last night. "Let's start looking."

They found Walter upstairs in Balpesh's study. The young knight lay blue-lipped and shivering where he had collapsed in front of the tall bookcase that stood between two shuttered windows. Walter's left hand was still clenched around the hilt of his heavy sword.

Randal hurried forward and went down to his knees on the floor beside his cousin.

"What are you doing up here?" he demanded, almost angrily. "You could have killed yourself just climbing those stairs."

"I heard someone calling my name," said Walter. His voice sounded faint and tired, but clear. "I thought it was you. And there was a light, floating in the air. . . . I followed it in here, but the room was empty."

Randal looked at his cousin. *Last night something spoke through Walter. If he followed something up here— maybe it's happened again.* "No," Randal said slowly, "I don't think the room is empty."

"What do you mean?" asked Lys.

"I should have known that the workroom wouldn't be far from the library," said Randal. He pointed at the bookcase. "Look there. What do you see?"

She followed the line of his finger. "A bookcase."

Randal nodded. "The only floor-to-ceiling bookcase in the whole tower."

"But it's standing against the outside of the tower," Lys objected. "The wall isn't thick enough to fit in a secret room!"

"A detail like that isn't likely to stop a master wizard," Randal explained. "He could have a permanent-illusion spell cast on this room so that it looks like that's an outside wall. Or he could have a portal there leading to a room that's buried fifty feet below the foundation of the tower. There are a hundred ways to hide a room. I don't know which one Balpesh used. But I'm certain the room is here. All I have to do is find it."

Randal got to his feet and began pulling books off the shelves, dropping volume after volume onto the floor with no regard for delicate illuminated illustrations or fine leather bindings. Soon he stood ankle-deep in drifted books, with the entire inside of the bookcase lying bare in front of him.

One spot in the wooden paneling looked darker than the rest, with an oily sheen to it, as though it had been touched many times. "That'll be the catch," he said. He reached out a hand toward the worn spot, then paused and drew back.

"Lys," he said, turning around to face her as he spoke. "Take Walter. Go down to the kitchen and wait for me there."

"What sort of friend do you think I am?" she said hotly. "I'm going to help you. You don't know what might be on the other side of that wall."

I don't know what's there, Randal thought. *But I can guess, and I wish it were almost anything else but what I think it is.* Aloud, he said, "I do know it's nothing you can help me with. Please, Lys. I want you and Walter safely out of the way before I open that door."

Walter pushed himself up to a half-sitting position with his good arm. His face was pale and haggard, with a bright flush of fever high up on his cheekbones, but his expression was stubborn. "I can't let you face trouble alone, Randy. What could I possibly say to my father afterward—or to yours?"

Randal bit his lip. *Don't worry,* he thought. *Unless Balpesh heals you, you won't live long enough to carry the tale to anyone.*

"Tell them I sent you away," he told his cousin. "Neither one of you can help me with this—and if what I suspect is true, somebody will have to get word to Master Madoc and the Regents of the Schola."

"What are you talking about?" Lys demanded.

"A demon is loose in the world, and Balpesh is trapped where he can't fight it." He looked at his two friends. "Lys," he said, "I have to free Balpesh.

100

If I can't—if anything goes wrong—you'll have to carry the tale to someone who can fight the demon and win."

"I'll tell Master Madoc," she said. "If I can."

"Swear it, Lys," he insisted. "Swear that if you get a bad feeling—if you get nervous or scared—you'll forget about me. Just get Walter out of here and run."

Walter gave a breathless laugh. "If things get that bad, Randal, I'll have to stay behind. I couldn't run as far as the front gate."

Lys looked from Randal to Walter and back again. "He's right," she said to Randal. "If I go, I'll have to leave him."

"I know," said Randal. His voice sounded tired and far away in his own ears. "Swear to it just the same."

"I swear I'll carry the news to Madoc," she said.

There's something she isn't saying, Randal thought, but he was too tired, and too weighed down by his own fear, to press her any further. "Then go," he said. "Take Walter, and wait for me downstairs."

He stood watching as she helped his cousin to his feet. Slowly, Lys and Walter made their way across the book-strewn room and out the door. Randal, standing immobile next to the bookcase, felt as if their departure had drained all the warmth from his body.

He shivered and leaned his forehead against the empty shelf in front of him. Then he straightened up again, and pressed his hand against the worn spot at the rear of the empty bookcase. He pushed,

101

and the paneling sagged inward. He heard a faint but distinct click. He pressed again, harder, and the secret door swung open.

Right through what should have been the outside wall of the tower, it swung. The moving bookcase revealed a room far larger than any room Randal had yet seen in the tower. This was surely the secret workroom that he had been seeking in vain for so long. Randal stepped through the open door.

The wizard's workroom glowed with a blue and eerie light. The illumination came from not one but two overlapping magic circles, laid out on the workroom floor like a pair of linked rings. Tall candles spaced around them were lit with small orange flames. Bitter-smelling incense burned in little copper pots, and the blue-gray smoke made slow, lazy curls in the still air.

In the center of each circle stood a wizard.

"Help me!" called the wizard in the left-hand circle—a tall, gray-bearded man in ceremonial robes of black velvet embroidered with magical symbols in gold and silver. "Break the circle so that I can destroy the demon!"

"No!" shouted the other wizard—also tall, also gray-bearded, also clad in ceremonial robes of black velvet trimmed in gold and silver. "No! Help me! *I* am Master Balpesh—*he* is the demon Eram!"

Randal looked from one wizard to the other. Each one stood imprisoned inside a magic circle, and each one held the other prisoner. Just as the circles themselves were intertwined, the wizard and the demon were locked in a deadly stalemate.

"Hurry!" commanded the wizard on the right. "Break the circle around me and set me free!"

"No, no!" cried the wizard on the left. "Free me from this circle, and we can fight the demon together."

"Don't listen to him!" cried the other wizard. "He'll destroy you!"

With every exchange, the two circles pulsed and glowed as the wizards tested their strength against the boundaries that held them prisoner. Randal looked from one wizard to the other, and saw that the two were entirely identical: every wrinkle on the face of one was matched on the face of the other. He could see no differences at all.

Why does it have to be me? Randal thought. *The last time I walked into a wizard's private workroom, I almost didn't come out again. This time . . . if I guess wrong, I might turn loose something far, far worse than Master Laerg could have ever been.*

Then, with a laugh that was almost a sob, the journeyman lifted his head and straightened his shoulders. *Why am I worried? If I guess wrong, I'll be dead. Even if I guess right, the demon may kill us both. And there's no other way to get my magic back. . . . No other way at all.*

He walked farther into the room, taking care not to touch the circles. Whichever one he chose, breaking it would be easy—a physical act. Anyone could do it, just by crossing the circle from the outside.

It was obvious to Randal that the wizard and the demon were evenly matched. Even the slightest advantage given to one would allow victory. *I have to choose,* he thought. *But I don't dare choose wrong.*

The storm still raged outside. From the open door to the library, Randal could hear the sounds of wind and rain. He walked all around the two wizards, in order to see if one of them looked different from another angle. Neither one did.

So this is what happens, Randal thought, *when you get a magical duel going on.* The illusory storm outside reflected the events inside those two interlocking magic circles, just as everything that had happened for the past week—the bandits on the road, the betrayal at the tourney, even the obstacles on the way to Balpesh's tower—had been caused by the presence of the demon.

The demon warps everything toward evil, he realized, *just by being here. If it gets free of the circle . . .*

He knew that he had to do something. The human wizard would have to eat and sleep sometime, but the demon, no matter how human it chose to look, had no such disadvantage. If the contest continued, then in the long run the demon would win.

And I can't allow that, thought Randal. *I survived a roomful of demons once, but that was by luck, not skill. Luck, and some help from three of the greatest wizards in the realm.*

The storm outside grew fiercer, and Randal knew that the two in the circles had begun attacking each other again.

I could free one of them, and trust to luck, Randal thought. *But with only one chance in two of guessing right . . . luck isn't something I can count on. Powerful*

105

magics are being cast here. You can't trust luck where magic is involved.

He knew that more than his own life was at stake. True, a wrong choice would mean his death, and a painful one at that. But the demon wouldn't stop with him. It would go on to kill Balpesh and Walter and Lys, as well. Then more, and more, throughout the kingdom. Randal couldn't guess where the killing would end.

Maybe Lys has already run for it, thought Randal. *Maybe someone will bring help.*

He shook his head. *You're dithering,* he told himself. *Not choosing is the same as making a choice.*

Very well, then. I'll free the one on the right.

He walked up to just outside the right-hand circle. "Yes, yes!" called the wizard inside. "Free me, so together we can destroy this demon!"

Or maybe I should free the one on the left.

Randal stepped closer to the intersection of the glowing boundaries. All that he needed to do was to put his hand through one circle or the other, and that circle would break.

He paused for a moment, turned to his right, and stretched out his hand.

IX.
Wizard and Demon

"NO!"

Randal froze, his fingers still a hair's breadth away from the flickering boundary of the magic circle.

The outcry had come from the entrance to the secret room. Randal turned, and saw two figures moving forward into the blue light that filled the chamber. One of them was Lys, and the other was his cousin Walter. The young knight carried his naked sword before him, and its edges gleamed in the magical light. Walter's eyes were fever bright, and he moved stiffly, but step by step he came forward until he faced the wizard in the right-hand circle.

"Demon," he said hoarsely, "if steel can harm you, my steel shall harm you!"

Randal drew in a sharp breath. *If Walter's right, I almost freed Eram instead of the wizard.*

"Don't touch the circle!" he shouted at his cousin. In the same breath Randal turned, and thrust his hand through the glittering boundary of the left-hand circle. The spell collapsed, and the wizard stepped free.

I hope I got it right this time, thought Randal.

"Help me now," the newly freed wizard said. "With your strength and mine together, we may—"

On the other side of the room, Lys cried out in horror. Randal looked in the direction of her shout, and saw the second wizard begin to twist and change, his body writhing, stretching into a man-shaped thing seven feet tall. Its hide was dead white, scarred and scabbed. The short white hair of its head grew down its spine like a mane. Wet fangs protruded from its mouth, and glittering claws studded its hands and feet. The demon Eram pressed against the bounds of the magic circle.

But Balpesh was tired and distracted from his task by the new arrivals. The circle in which he had imprisoned his foe flickered. As Randal watched, the demon raised its long arms, pushed against the circle that surrounded it, and broke through.

The wizard Balpesh lifted his hand and shot off a fireball that set the demon's hair afire. Smoke billowed upward toward the ceiling of the secret chamber.

The demon roared and thrust its paw at Balpesh. The wizard countered with a magical gesture of his own, but nevertheless staggered back a pace from the impact of whatever Eram had thrown at him. The demon surged forward, howling, toward Randal and the master wizard.

Behind the unearthly shape, Walter raised his sword left-handed. "Creature of evil!" he shouted. "Do you dare turn your back on a knight?"

He brought the sword forward and down. The heavy blade took Eram in the back of the skull, and cut downward through the scaly body all the way to the demon's belly. Eram laughed and turned around, ripping the blade from Walter's hand with the motion. The demon reached for the now-weaponless knight. Razor-tipped claws spread wide, ready to rip Walter's heart from his body.

A candlestick came sailing out of the corner to smash against the back of the demon's skull. Eram turned. Lys stood in the far corner of the workroom, her upraised hand now empty. The demon shook its head, snarled, and turned its attention back to the knight.

"You're a wizard!" Balpesh shouted at Randal. "Join your strength to mine and we can stop the demon!"

"I can't do magic!" Randal shouted back. "Not without—" He never got a chance to finish the sentence. Balpesh turned on him with a furious yell.

"You fool, you had *better* do magic! Come on now—a lightning bolt, both of us together, one, two, three, go!"

Randal threw a lightning bolt, the most powerful he had ever summoned, putting into it all the frustration and anger of the past magicless months. Balpesh did the same, in a display of dazzling fire, so that the master and the journeyman wizard formed the base of a triangle of brilliant white light, with the demon prince at its apex. The lightning surrounded the demon, but did not touch it. The thing laughed and took another step toward the two wizards.

Balpesh saw what was happening. "The demon

has shielded itself!" he cried out. "Cast your spell at the sword instead!"

Together, Randal and Balpesh spoke the words. Lightning played over the sword protruding from the demon's guts. A violet glow surrounded the weapon from point to pommel as the steel blade carried magical fire past the demon's shield-spell and deep into its body.

The demon writhed and twisted toward the two wizards, blue-white fire crackling around it. Thunder roared in the air, shaking the stones. A smell of burnt hair filled the room. The demon began to scorch and shrivel. Balpesh called out the spell of portal opening, to create a gate through which the demon could be forced back to its own world.

But the master wizard was almost exhausted by his long ordeal in the secret room—the portal wavered, and started to fail. Hastily, Randal invoked the spell of steadying, and gave his strength to the exhausted older man. The demon fell away from them, into a place between worlds, back to the demonic plane. The crack in reality remained for a moment in the stinking air. Then the gate fell in on itself and closed.

Balpesh stumbled over to a chair, and sat down heavily. "That was a near thing," he said, "the nearest thing that I've seen in a long time. It could have been bad, if all of you hadn't shown up." He looked at Randal. "Now, then—what's all this about not being able to do magic?"

Before Randal could answer, a shriek from Lys cut through the air in the secret room.

"Walter!"

Randal spun around, and froze in shock. The young knight lay unmoving on the floor of the secret workroom. Frothy red blood trickled from his mouth, and his head lay in a pool of bright red foam.

All Balpesh's weariness seemed to vanish in an instant. He rose and strode over to the fallen knight.

"Help him," Randal said quietly as the master wizard knelt and touched Walter's neck. "Please."

"It may be too late already," Balpesh replied. He stood up again, his robes swirling around him. "But if it is not—you, girl, fetch water. And you—" he pointed at Randal, "take that chest there in the corner. Follow me."

The wizard turned back to Walter's still form. Bubbles were forming outside the young fighter's mouth, but there were no other signs of life. Balpesh held one hand out, palm up, and said *"Veni!"* in a voice of command.

Lys had already headed downstairs to the well. Randal, bending to pick up the chest of supplies, saw his cousin's body rise from the floor where it had been lying and begin to float from the room, face up and feet first. Balpesh followed behind, one hand resting lightly on the young man's forehead, chanting something too low for Randal to hear.

The little procession went out of the workroom, through the study, and up the stairway. Before, Randal had needed a candle to climb the spiral stairs. Now he was able to walk swiftly and surely upward, following the golden glow that surrounded the master wizard. Lys came behind Randal, lugging a heavy bucket of water. All of them made their way to the topmost chamber, where Randal and Lys had begun their search only the day before.

Balpesh brought the wounded knight hovering above the wide bed and, still chanting, lowered him down onto the quilted coverlet. Walter was deathly still and pale.

"He is nearly done," said the master wizard. "If this man is to have a chance at all, one of you will have to give him some of your life force. It will be dangerous, for if he dies, then whoever is linked with him will die as well."

Randal drew a deep breath. There was no question, he knew, about what his cousin would have done if their positions had been reversed.

"I'll do it," he said. In the same instant, he heard Lys's voice saying, "Take me."

"Well, well, such loyalty," said Balpesh, sounding both weary and amused at the same time. He looked first at Lys and then at Randal.

"I'll take you," he said at last to the journeyman wizard. "You are of his blood, I think. That should make matters easier. Lie beside him on the bed."

Randal stretched out next to Walter on the coverlet. Lying there, Randal felt calm and very, very tired. He looked at Walter. The young knight, although bloodstained and pale, also looked peaceful, and the signs of pain were gone from his face.

Somewhere across the room, Randal heard the lid of the chest being opened. Balpesh began to chant again, a low, monotonous sound. Randal listened closely.

The words were in the Old Tongue, the language of conjuration. Randal had learned to speak it at the Schola, and now he listened with growing concern to exactly what Balpesh was saying. The charm was one to take the blood from Randal's body and give it to his cousin.

He's going to steal my blood! Randal thought in panic—even though it was Balpesh working the spell, the intent came too close to what Laerg had almost done to him. He tried to rise, but his limbs were too heavy. He couldn't move. His eyes wouldn't open.

No! he thought. *I can't let myself go to sleep. I have to see what's happening!* He struggled to stay awake, but the darkness of sleep closed around him.

Something hummed near his face and head—a large fly, Randal supposed, like the ones in the stable of the Basilisk Inn. The fly touched Randal's nose, and he swatted at it without opening his eyes. But the sun was bright against his closed lids, and the air was warm. *I might as well get up,* Randal thought, *and have a look around.*

He found himself wrapped in his cloak, lying under a hedgerow. He stood and stretched, and walked out into the road. Two men rode toward him, leading a third horse by its bridle. One of the fellows was short and fat, and dressed like a merchant. The other was a burly man, armed and armored.

The men rode without looking either right or left. As they came closer, Randal recognized their faces. One was the young knight, Sir Louis, who had died

113

in the assault at the inn, and the other was the murdered merchant, whose name Randal had never known. Dark blood clotted on the wound in Sir Louis's forehead, and the merchant still wore the strangler's cord embedded in the plump flesh of his neck.

I'm dreaming, thought Randal. *This has to be a dream.*

The horses drew abreast of him and passed on. The dead men sat unmoving, as if they had been carved from wood. The riderless horse paced between them. *The empty saddle is for me,* Randal thought. *All I have to do is climb on, and I can ride.*

Randal fought against the urge to mount the horse. He stood and watched the men go. Before long the horsemen passed from sight as the road entered some woods. Randal began to walk down the road in the direction they had gone.

Abruptly, he looked up. The road ended twenty feet ahead in unmarked forest. Randal looked behind him. The road extended no more than twenty feet in that direction before it, too, ended in forest. Randal turned forward again. The road ended fifteen feet ahead of him, not twenty as he had thought.

Randal felt a chill race down his spine. A glance behind showed that the forest had approached to within ten feet of his back while he wasn't looking. Randal closed his eyes and counted to five. When he looked around again, the road had vanished. He was deep in the trackless woods.

A sudden wind blew through the treetops high above, tossing the upper branches, but sending no draft of air down into the dappled shadows where Randal waited. He looked in the direction from which the wind had come, and saw a strange, twisted tree growing a little apart from the rest.

He felt a great longing in his heart. The tree called to him, pulling him closer almost against his will. As he drew near, he saw that the tree was strange indeed. Three different kinds of leaves grew from its twisted limbs. Randal realized that three trees had grown up here in the same spot, intertwining so that they merged into a single trunk: an oak, a rowan, and an ash.

Randal walked around the interwoven trunk. On the far side, he found proof that he had not been the first to pass this way. The wood of the rowan tree bore the unmistakable signs of an ax. The ax's edge had bitten deep, cutting large chips from the trunk, but that had been long ago, because the bark had started to grow again over the wound.

The wind rustled again in the trees, and a beautiful, melodious voice spoke from behind Randal.

"You fought me in your world. Now fight me in mine."

Randal turned. The demon Eram stood before him, a tall figure gleaming brilliant white in the sunlight that pierced the forest.

For a moment, time froze. *Beautiful,* Randal kept thinking, in something like despair. *In its own world, a demon prince is beautiful beyond belief.* Then the demon leapt at Randal, seized him, and the two fell to the forest floor.

Randal hit the ground full on his back, and kept

on falling, passing through the ground into a dark place, with the demon clawing at his throat.

Dream! he thought. *This is a dream!*

But dreams don't hurt, the answer came, *and this one does. It hurts bad.*

Randal called up light in the dark place, using the spells that had lain unpracticed for half a year. A light came to him—not a blinding glare, but a fitful glimmer, and what he saw almost made him wish for the dark. The demon was on him, tearing at his chest, and white fangs gleamed like ivory needles only inches from his face.

Only the trained reflexes he'd carried away from the practice yard of Castle Doun saved him from having those fangs buried in his skull. When the demon attacked, Randal blocked with his left arm, and now his forearm was jammed up under the demon's jaw, keeping that living nightmare from putting an end to him.

I can't hold off a demon bare-handed, thought Randal. *I have to do something, or I'm going to die.*

He threw a lightning bolt. It sputtered and fizzled when it hit the demon's body. Eram laughed—a musical, bell-toned sound—and raked at the young wizard's back and belly with knife-edged claws.

If you die in a dream, do you die for real? And in the demon's world, does it make any difference?

Randal was still falling, falling with the demon on top of him, snapping at him. Eram's mouth opened impossibly wide, and a long, crimson tongue flicked out.

116

I can't let it get me, thought Randal. *A demon prince, fed with a wizard's blood . . . who knows what it might do?*

There was only one thing left to try. Drawing on all his reserves of strength, Randal called up a fireball—not on the invulnerable body of the demon prince, but on himself.

The flames came, with pain worse than he had ever experienced, worse than the pain of the claws raking his back, worse than grasping a sword blade, worse than anything, until the flame red was replaced with black, and he awoke.

Randal lay on the bed in the top chamber of Balpesh's tower. Lys sat cross-legged on the coverlet at the foot of the bed, her lute in her hands, playing a soft, sad tune. And as she played, she sang:

> "His hound is to the hunting gone,
> His hawk to fetch the wild fowl home,
> His lady's taken another mate,
> So we may make our breakfast sweet."

Outside the tower, dawn was breaking, and light from the rising sun caught the lute strings, turning them red-gold in the shadows. Lys looked up from her playing

"You're awake," she said.

"Yes," said Randal. "And hungry, too. Where is everybody?"

"It's not surprising that you're hungry," Lys told him. "You've been asleep since before this time yesterday. As for Walter and Balpesh, they're down in the kitchen, making breakfast."

Randal turned toward the edge of the bed. He ached all over. "Can you tell me what happened?"

"Besides what you already know?" asked Lys. "I didn't understand much."

"Tell me what you saw."

Lys put aside the lute. "Well, Balpesh put you and Walter here, and he chanted until way past dark. I lit candles when the sun went down. All the time, Walter kept looking better, and you kept looking worse. Then all the water in the bucket I brought vanished, and Walter woke up. I took him downstairs and got him dressed, and when I got back, Balpesh was working over you. After a while, he said you'd get better, and to feed you when you got up. So I stayed, and you woke up, and here we are. Let's go see about getting you something to eat."

Randal stood. He felt weak and light-headed; Lys saw that he was swaying, and came to support him. They walked down the stairs together and entered the kitchen, where bunches of dried herbs hung from the ceiling beams and a fire burned in the hearth. Two fresh loaves of bread lay cooling on the sideboard, and Walter sat at the large table, dressed in a clean tunic, digging into a large plate of scrambled eggs.

He looked up as Randal entered the room. "Your friend is a good cook, I'll give him that."

"That's what you need more than anything else," Balpesh said from his seat at the fireside. "Good food for good healing. For both of you."

Randal sat down at the table, and Lys brought him a plate of eggs and a cup of milk. He ate hungrily for several minutes, then took a long drink of the milk and set the cup aside. "I'm glad it's all over," he said. "For a while there, I didn't think any of us were going to come out alive—even last night, my dreams were still full of death and disaster."

Walter glanced up from his own meal. "Dreaming again?" he asked, looking concerned. "I hope it wasn't anything like the last nightmare you had."

"I don't know," said Randal slowly. "It was very strange. And my dreams usually do mean something." Seeing that Walter continued to regard him with a worried expression, he went on to tell everything that he had seen. "It was all so real," he said finally. "I don't understand how the fireball I cast on myself could hurt so much and still not kill me."

Balpesh spoke up again for the first time in several minutes. "Sometimes a dream is only a dream," he said. "You never cast a fireball, you only dreamed of it. You were safely at rest through it all. Had you truly been fighting a demon, you would not have come out of the struggle unscathed. What you experienced was just a disturbing nightmare, no more."

Master Madoc said all dreams have meaning, Randal thought, but he decided to let the matter pass. He ate his fill of eggs and fresh bread and cool milk, and soon found himself feeling better, and full of more energy than he had had in months.

When Randal had finished his breakfast, Master Balpesh rose from the bench by the hearth and beckoned to him. "Now," said the master wizard, "you and I have some work to do—repairing the bridge and clearing the rest of the path back to town. Can you work a levitation spell?"

"I know how," said Randal, "but I've never done a really big one."

Balpesh nodded. "Then this is an excellent time to practice. Come with me."

Randal rose from the table, and walked out with Master Balpesh through the silent farmstead and down the path to the ravine. The morning sun coming over the mountains cast a clear yellow light on the jagged ends of the broken bridge.

"The first warning that the demon was near was when this bridge collapsed," Balpesh said. "Now we have to raise it again."

The day was beautiful, and the air was warm. One by one, the master wizard called the broken pieces of stone out of the gorge so far below. Randal found that he wasn't able to reach that far with his magic, and contented himself with smoothing the spider-web of cracks on the bridge's surface.

The sun stood at high noon by the time the last stone settled into place. Then, as Randal and Balpesh stood together on the center of the span, the wizard spoke again.

"There's one more thing you ought to know," he said.

"What's that?"

"Your friends are dead. You freed the wrong wizard."

X.

Journeyman and Wizard

I FREED THE wrong wizard.

Randal stood on the center span of the bridge and stared at Balpesh. The master wizard was smiling at him, but his eyes were wrong—dead black and fathomless, with no white showing.

Demon eyes.

The old man's skin split and fell away, and Eram emerged like some foul butterfly from its human cocoon. The demon prince started forward across the stones of the bridge, an evil presence that seemed to suck all the good out of the world as it came.

And there's no one left to stop it, thought Randal. *No one but me. Was this what my dream meant, after all?*

Balpesh had said that the dream had no meaning—but Balpesh had died in the secret workroom, and the demon had worn his face thereafter. *And he wanted me to forget the dream. Something in the dream was important, but I can't remember . . .*

Eram laughed, enjoying Randal's fear, and stretched out its ivory claws. "Now, little wizard, I'll have your blood."

Randal stood as if rooted to the spot. *I have to remember,* he thought, *or I'm going to die.*

Then he did remember, as the razor-edged claws made their first delicate nick in the flesh of his throat. *That was the answer Eram wanted me to forget. I have to die to kill him.*

And he cast a spell, using the same fireball that had served him in his nightmare—throwing it not at the demon, but at the bridge beneath Eram's feet. The stone cracked with the heat, and split apart along the cracks. Randal felt the center span of the bridge tilt under his feet. Eram howled and sprang back, but Randal held on to him with his arms. Then the whole world seemed to fall away from under them with a noise like thunder, and the bridge collapsed into the chasm, taking Randal and the demon with it as it went. Randal clasped Eram close while he chanted the spell of negation, so neither he nor the demon could work magic to save themselves.

And Randal fell, at last, out of the dream and back into reality.

He lay once again in Balpesh's bedchamber. Dark night filled the room, broken by the yellow light of candles. Faces looked down at him: Lys, his cousin Walter, and Balpesh.

The master wizard looked near done in with exhaustion. "We almost lost you," he said. "But you're back."

"The demon," said Randal. "Eram. I saw him in my dream. . . ." Haltingly, for his voice was weak and his chest and ribs hurt him whenever he drew a breath, Randal told Balpesh everything that had happened since the healing spell began. He finished, finally, by saying, "I still don't know if the demon in my dream was real."

The wizard nodded. "All too real. The spell we used in the workroom to send the demon back to its own plane of existence wasn't quite powerful enough. Eram had time to prepare a gateway back to this world. If you hadn't met the demon on its own plane of existence and stopped it there, it might well have come back into our world and after all of us."

"So it wasn't really a dream, after all," said Randal.

"Not in the way most people know dreams," Balpesh told him. "You appear to have a natural talent for slipping between the various planes of existence, and in this case it served you—in fact, it served all of us—well. I'm in your debt for my rescue. Let your wounds finish healing. Then we can talk about what happened here."

Randal frowned, not certain he'd heard the wizard right. "Wounds? What wounds?"

It was Walter who answered. The young knight was still pale, but his face was no longer marred by fever and pain. The only outward reminder of his injury was the white linen sling that supported his right arm. "Right now, cousin," Walter said to Randal, "you're wearing more bandages than I am."

"That explains why I hurt all over," Randal murmured. "What happened?"

Walter shook his head. "I don't know. The last

thing I remember is looking into the door of that secret room and seeing you reach out toward the ugliest creature I've ever seen, and it was laughing. I struck it, and then I woke up in here with a clear head while something we couldn't see was clawing you to pieces."

"You never went downstairs like I asked you to," said Randal. He laughed in spite of the fact that laughter tore at the claw marks on his bandaged chest. "See if I try to keep you out of trouble anymore. But I'll forgive you this time, since if you hadn't picked out the demon . . ."

He let the sentence hang.

Balpesh smiled at Randal. "It's all very well to speak of a wizard's keen and subtle powers of observation," he said. "But the illusion the demon cast was *meant* to deceive a wizard. That same illusion had no effect on a man like your cousin."

"Lucky for me that it didn't," said Randal, with a sigh.

"You all did extremely well," said Balpesh. "Without Walter's blade inside the demon's defenses, or the candlestick which Lys threw, distracting its attention at a crucial moment, I doubt that any of us would be here. But especially you, Randal. Your magic, added to mine, is what sent that foul creature back to its home."

"I'm still confused," Lys said. The elder wizard turned to face her, his expression inviting her to continue.

"For example, how was it that I was able to climb into the tower through a window? Randal said that this place would have protection spells all over it. If I were a master wizard, I'd guard my home so that strangers couldn't get in."

"And this tower is guarded, with spells powerful and deadly," Balpesh replied. "But they are triggered by evil intent. Had you come meaning to steal my spoons, I daresay you wouldn't have found the entry so easy. But instead," he continued, "your motives couldn't have been better. You sought help for another. But come, we should let Randal rest so that my healing spells can work on him. There will be much time for talk tomorrow."

"One more thing," Randal said from the bed. "In my dream, I saw a strange tree—an oak, an ash, and a rowan, all growing together as one. What does that mean?"

"If I were going to make a guess, I'd say that you were looking at the friendship among you, Lys and Walter. Walter, strong and reliable, is the oak; Lys, slender and resilient, is the ash; and you are the rowan, a tree of magic."

"Someone tried to cut down the rowan," Randal said. "I saw the ax marks. What does it mean?"

"That's because Laerg nearly cut you down," Balpesh said, "although you have recovered nicely. What the vision means, now, is something else again. Clearly the three of you are destined to play some part together, but what that part might be, I can't even guess." The wizard paused. "And those are enough questions for tonight. Sleep now, and we will talk more in the morning."

Randal leaned back in the bed, and fell asleep. This time, he had no dreams.

The next few days went by quickly as Randal recovered from his combat with the demon prince. The marks of the demon's claws soon faded from Randal's chest and shoulders, leaving no scars behind—a tribute to Balpesh's healing skills. The master wizard also took the opportunity to instruct Randal in the basics of the healer's art, teaching him the spells to stop bleeding and close wounds, to lower fevers and ease pain.

"Healing is the greatest of the arts of the wizard," said Balpesh one day as he guided Randal through a practice session in the healing spells, "even though not many of the Schola-trained chose to follow it."

The master wizard looked at the scar on Randal's palm. "Do you want me to do away with that?" he asked. "It's quite simple, really."

"No," Randal replied after a moment's thought. "It's ugly, and it hurts, but I want to keep it. To remind me that choices always have their consequences."

The older wizard smiled at the answer, as if Randal had passed a secret test. "Come then. It's time to repair my broken bridge and set you and your friends back on your way."

Randal and Balpesh left the workroom, going out through the wizard's study and down the spiral staircase to the storeroom at the bottom of the tower. The door to the outside stood open, and Lys sat on the doorstep, playing her lute and singing.

" 'Well met, well met, my own true love,
Well met, well met,' said he.
'I've just returned from the salt, salt sea,
And it's all for the sake of thee.' "

Beyond Lys, out in the farmyard, Randal saw his cousin Walter practicing with the heavy sword, swinging it one-handed through a series of blows at an invisible opponent. The shoulder that had once been broken beyond repair moved freely and easily, and the young knight looked well on the way to regaining all his old strength and speed.

Balpesh turned to Randal. "One more thing, before we start to work on the bridge." The master wizard pointed at a stack of chests and boxes huddled against one wall. "Go look in that small box on the top there—the locking spell isn't a particularly difficult one."

Randal went over to the boxes and tried the lock on the one Balpesh had indicated. As the master wizard had said, the spell holding the chest closed was a simple one; no more complex than the charms most apprentices in the Schola used to keep their personal belongings safe from casual tampering. Randal undid the spell after only a few moments' concentration, and the lid of the chest rose up to reveal a folded robe made of plain black cloth.

"Put it on," said Balpesh.

Randal slipped the robe on over his tunic and

hose. The wide-sleeved black garment hung down to mid-calf, and had deep pockets on either side, much like the robes apprentice wizards wore back at the Schola. This robe, however, was made of much heavier cloth, and had a hood that could be pulled up over the wearer's head for protection against cold or rain.

This is a journeyman's robe, Randal thought. He looked into the chest again, and saw something more: a small, leatherbound book that had lain hidden under the black cloth of the robe. He picked the book up and opened it. The handwriting inside was his own.

"My spell-book," he said. "I left it at the Schola." He looked over at Balpesh. "How did these things come to be here?"

"On the day when I put on master's robes," said the older wizard, "I put aside my journeyman's clothing. I put my old robe away and locked the chest with a simple charm. Then I spoke a spell over it so that on the day the box was opened again, I would find not only my old robe, but also the one other object most needed by the journeyman who would wear it. For fifty years and more, that box has lain unopened, waiting for the day when the robe would be needed again. At last, the day has come."

"Then I'm truly a journeyman?" asked Randal. "When I saw what you wrote in your journal, I thought that you didn't intend to let me use magic again."

The master wizard looked at him gravely. "As you suspected, I knew of your troubles and watched your progress as you traveled. But I was still uncertain, when the demon came, whether or not I should give you permission. It was never so much the matter of the sword that concerned me, as a fear that learning so much from Master Laerg might have corrupted you. But you kept your vow not to use magic, and you fought the demon at great risk to yourself on our plane and on its own."

He smiled at Randal. "And now, journeyman, we have a bridge to repair."

Randal slipped the spell-book into the pocket of his robe and followed Balpesh out into the farmyard. Lys stopped singing as they stepped past her onto the doorstep, and Walter abandoned his sword practice to come up for a closer look at his cousin.

Randal stood patiently as Walter gave him a thorough inspection. Finally the young knight smiled. "I think I've lost my squire," he said. "I'm glad for you, Randal, but I'm going to miss you out on the road."

"I'd like to stick with you for a while," said Randal, "but there's not much magic to be learned following the tourneys. And before we go anywhere, I have to help Master Balpesh rebuild the bridge."

Walter sheathed his sword. "I think I want to watch this," he said. "Ever since I heard that you went off to be a wizard, I've wanted to see you do some magic, and this is my first chance."

"I'm coming, too," said Lys. "Every time I let you out of my sight something terrible happens."

Master Balpesh laughed gently. "Then together it is," he said. Together they walked down the path to the ravine, going over the gap in the high hills around the farm and down the stone steps cut into the face of the rock. In the clear light of midmorning, the ruined bridge over the mountain gorge made a lonely and forsaken sight.

Master Balpesh frowned at the wreckage. "Tell me, Randal, have you ever watched stonemasons build a bridge?"

"No," Randal admitted.

"Then let this be your first lesson as a journeyman," said the master wizard. "On your travels, take note of everything—not just the odd bits and pieces of magic you may encounter. If you understand how a thing is done without magic, then you will know how to do it with magic, as well."

Balpesh pointed toward the ravine and the ruined heaps of stone on either side. "Consider bridges," he went on. "When stonemasons make bridges, first they build a wooden platform below the span to hold the stones until the work is done. Now I want you to make a magical platform for me, using your levitation spell to hold each stone in place until the keystone is in. Once that stone is in place, the world, and not magic, will support the bridge."

Randal nodded, and checked his spell-book. Yes, the words of the levitation spell were there, just as he had copied them down during Master Tarn's lecture. He tucked the spell-book back into his pocket, and strode up to the edge of the ravine. After taking a moment to calm his mind, he spoke the words, made the gestures, and thought the thoughts that would bend the world to his will.

"Fiat!" he concluded, and felt the gratifying mental warmth of a spell that had gone right. He nodded to Master Balpesh, and then stood at the gap, watching as the master wizard used magic to cut stones from the cliff face below. Blocks of stone floated free and rose to the level of the bridge. The blocks settled into place one by one, lying smoothly together on the invisible framework that Randal had constructed.

At last Balpesh fitted the keystone into the arch and pronounced, "It is finished."

Randal ended his levitation spell, and sat down heavily on the ground. He bowed his head down on his knees for a moment, breathing heavily—the spell had taken more out of him than he'd expected.

"You're out of practice," said Balpesh kindly, "and your struggles with the demon left you drained as well. Your strength and magical reserves will grow as you work more magic and gain experience."

The master wizard looked at Walter. "Have you seen your cousin do enough magic now?" he asked in a mild tone, and then shook his head without waiting for an answer. "Ah, but you didn't see what he did. You believe that the bridge could not have been built in this fashion without his help—but you believe with your mind, not your heart."

Balpesh turned to Randal. "Here is a spell that I am sure you know. Take these"—he pulled two acorns from the pocket of his robe—"and regrow my trees."

Randal took the acorns, weighing them in his

hands. Then he walked over to where the pine tree had once stood. He put the acorn in the little patch of bare dirt that nestled in the rocks. Then he walked across the bridge, feeling its steadiness and rejoicing in the sense of accomplishment that the creation of something so practical gave him.

On the far side of the bridge, where only a stump remained, he placed the second acorn in a crack in the broken wood. Then he retreated to the center of the span and spoke the words of growth and life that Master Laerg had first shown him in the library of the Schola. While he watched, a green shoot appeared from each of the acorns, and then—as twenty years of growth passed in a single minute—the shoots became saplings, and then young trees full of leaves, their roots firmly bound to the crevices in the rocks. The twin oak trees were pleasant and green, and their leaves whispered in the cool breeze that rose from the river so far below.

Randal walked back to his friends on the road to Balpesh's tower.

"Well done, Randal," the master wizard said. Randal smiled, even though working this spell so soon after helping rebuild the bridge had left him almost exhausted. But far more gratifying to him than Balpesh's praise was the look of wonder in Walter's eyes, and Lys's proud smile.

A few days later, Randal stood once more with Lys and Walter on the near side of the bridge. All three of the young people were dressed again for traveling.

"I'm heading for Cingestoun," said Randal. "There's a university there, and a library where I can spend a restful week or so poking around the scrolls and manuscripts."

"And I'm going with you," Lys said. "You need someone to keep you out of trouble."

Randal smiled. "I don't suppose I have any choice in the matter." He turned to his cousin. "How about you, Walter?" he asked. "We can go as far as Tattinham together, at least. Before you go anywhere else, you have to find out where Sir Guillaume left your horses and armor."

"And maybe you can find out where Sir Reginald went, as well," said Lys. "Because if he was the one who tried to kill you—"

"I have business to settle with Reginald," agreed Walter, "but my debt to Master Balpesh comes first." The young knight laughed. "I made the mistake of asking him if there was anything that I could do to repay him for healing me. There was. 'A little favor,' he called it."

"What did Balpesh ask you to do?" Randal asked.

"I have to return a book that he borrowed from the Hermit of the Western Isles," said Walter. He shook his head. "Minstrels sing of quests that were simpler—no one's traveled from Brecelande to the Western Isles in over a hundred years, and I thought the Hermit was only a legend."

Randal thought of his dream and the magical tree that had been three trees twined into one. "Do you need a wizard along?" he asked.

"No," said Walter. "This is something that I have to finish on my own."

"You'll do well, I know it," Randal told him. "And we'll travel together again someday—until then, we all have our own roads to follow."

His heart was light as he stepped out onto the broad stone bridge. *I have my magic back,* he thought happily, *Walter has the healing he risked so much for, and the whole world is open for us to explore.*

Together they started down out of the mountains into the bright new day.